FOR KIP AND VAL

THE CEDARVILLE SHOP AND THE WHEELBARROW SWAP

Bridget Krone

TABLE OF CONTENTS

NAMES

My name is Boipelo, which means *proud*. If proud is that quiet, warm feeling you carry deep in your heart, when you know you've been a part of something good, then maybe it is the right name for me. I didn't always think so, but now that I have had first-hand experience of how miracles can happen, I do.

I live in Cedarville in the Eastern Cape, in South Africa. It's a small village between two bigger towns, Matatiele and Kokstad. When I stand in the wide main street of my village and look west towards Matatiele, I can see the big blue mountains called the Drakensberg. My teacher, Mrs. Jafta, told us that Drakensberg means the "Mountains of Dragon"—and those mountains do look like the spikes on a dragon's back.

But the mountain behind our village does not look like a dragon's back. It's a big soft shape and covered with grass so it looks like the rump of a horse when it gets its furry winter coat. The slopes are green in summer. But soon after we've had our first frost in May, the grass turns the color of pale straw and in the winter, veld fires sometimes sweep over its slopes, and the mountain goes black. We just call it Cedarville Mountain and the wide flat veld area that stretches out in front of the village, where sheep and cattle graze, we've named the Cedarville Flats.

I live with my father and my grandmother in *Khorong Koali Park*, which is that part of the village closest to the river. When you grow up with names, you think they are easy to say. We speak both Sesotho and isiXhosa in this village and both languages have a lot of clicks. Once a visitor from London came to stay in my friend Potso's house, and we had to teach her the clicks so I know some people find them difficult. She also called the place where we live *Korrong Ko-Arlie Park* so it sounded like a place where koala bears might live. So Potso made her practice saying it with the right Sesotho pronunciation, *Khorong Kwa-dee, Khorong Kwa-dee* until she got it right.

"But why's it got an *l* in it when it should have a *d*?" she complained.

"For the same reason that the River Thames is spelled T-H-A-M-E-S not T-E-M-S," said Potso's mother, because for once Potso couldn't think of a good answer.

Anyway I'm getting off the point. What I really want to say is that a park should have green shady trees, grass, and birdsong. But here in Khorong Koali Park, we don't have those things; we have dust, weeds, thin dogs, and litter. Sometimes plastic bags flutter up from the ground and cling to fences and the small stunted peach trees like the one we have in our yard. Even the name *peach* doesn't describe the small, hard, green fruit those trees bear in spring. They give you a bad tummy ache—as if you've eaten stones.

The families in Khorong Koali Park live squeezed into small two-room houses that were built after we got our new government in 1994. Maybe when apartheid ended, people were in a rush to do things differently and these houses do look and feel like someone built them in a hurry. The walls are thin and cracked and the only reason many roofs don't blow away in the August winds is the blocks of concrete that hold them in place. Some houses have about twelve people under one roof. We joke that the houses are so small that people's feet protrude outside—like a tall person whose legs hang over a mattress when they are sleeping. But there are only three of us living in ours: my father, my grandmother, and myself.

Then there's the Umzimvubu River; more proof that things don't always get the right names. Umzimvubu means "place of the hippopotamus" but though no one I know has ever seen a hippopotamus there. But if you sit for a long time under a willow tree with your fishing line in the muddy water, you might see a legavaan lizard as it slides into the river and possibly a brown hammerkop bird on the bank. You will also probably hear the call of a fish-eagle high in the sky and you might see bits of broken crab shells, which the otters spit out. You have to be very quiet if you want to see an otter; they don't like noise. And my friend Potso and I make a lot of noise when we go to the river, so we have never seen one.

If we run fast and cut through Mr. Van Zyl's farm, we can get to the river in about ten minutes. We sing and fool around in the water; sometimes we fish for carp and, if we are bored, we dig clay from holes in the river bank and make little animals, mostly oxen with big horns or cows.

Once we made our own cigarette out of an old kha-ki-bos stem, which we stuffed with dried willow leaves. When we lit it, the whole thing burst into flames before we could take a drag so we threw it in the river and ran home. Potso had a blister on his finger from that burn. It was not one of our best ideas.

Sometimes I think back to the time when I did have a good idea; the time I read about the magic that can come from something as small as a red paperclip—and I wonder where those ideas come from and why they come to some of us and not others. I still don't understand it, but I do know this: it didn't turn out as I'd hoped in the beginning; it was a lot harder than I imagined, but there was magic there that I cannot explain.

MINCE

The day that this story started was just an ordinary Friday. I'd arrived home from school and found pap in a pot on the paraffin stove and amasi in a small enamel dish on the shelf. If cars and tractors run on Castrol GTX, then I run on this cold maize meal porridge and sour milk; it fills the hole in my tummy, and it's what I eat every day. I was so hungry that day, I just ate standing up.

While I ate, I dug in the pocket of my school trousers and fished out a phone. It wasn't mine. It belonged to Potso who'd got it from his cousin for twenty rand. We only realized why it was so cheap when we tried to get it to work: the battery went flat so quickly, and, although we fed it all the tiny bits of airtime we could afford, that phone never rang or received a single message. Then it fell out of Potso's pocket into a bucket of water while he was rinsing out his school uniform and died completely. I thought that if I could just get the back off and dry out all the parts, I might get it working again. I was jabbing the back cover with a fork when I heard my grandmother calling for me outside in the yard.

I'd seen her when I raced home from school but she'd been fast asleep in her chair under the peach tree, wrapped in a blanket, supposedly checking that thieves didn't steal the wet washing that hung over the fence. It was May and the weather was turning bitterly cold so the washing took a long time to dry.

"Boi!"

I'd just managed to pry off the back cover of the phone so I ignored her.

"Boipelo!"

My grandmother's English name is Patience and although I'd never say it out loud, I think her name should be *Cedarville Mountain* because of the way she looms over me, just like the mountain, every day of my life. I call her Makhulu, which means *big mother* and she has been beside me since the day I was born. My mother died in childbirth and so my grandmother moved into the house to look after me. She takes her job seriously. Nothing I eat, wear, say or do escapes her notice. I don't know how she does it, because she's almost blind.

When I looked up, she was standing in the doorway, leaning heavily on her walking stick.

"Boipelo Seku, are you deaf?"

When I complained to my father about her bad temper, he said that I'd be irritable too if all my joints ached and I could hardly see. Her spectacles are so thick, they look as if they are made from the bottoms of Coke bottles—but I wasn't sure they still worked. She was always wearing her clothes inside-out. Sometimes she tried to put her mug of tea on a table, missed the table, and the tea crashed to the floor.

She pointed under her bed where I was sitting.

"There's a pile of old magazines that the library Auntie gave me. I need someone to read to me while I sit outside watching the washing."

"Can I do it later?"

"Later? When is this time *later?*"

I got to my knees to look under the bed. I had to drag my foam mattress out. I put it there during the day and slide it out at night to sleep. There was a pile of old *You* magazines pushed against the wall. I pulled one out and followed my grandmother back out into the yard.

I got a piece of old cardboard to sit on—so my school pants didn't get dirty—and held the magazine up where I hoped she could see it. It was very old. The date on the top said December 2006. I hadn't even been born in 2006 so it was no wonder Auntie Shirley from the library threw them out.

"What do you want me to read?" I asked.

She stabbed at the cover with her crooked finger, and I turned to page eighty-five and began reading an article called "25 Festive Ideas for Mince."

"While most people think of mincemeat as everyday fare," I began, "the possibilities of using it for festive occasions and family get-togethers are endless. From burgers to bolognese, there's little to beat its versatility..."

It's very hard to ask a boy who has only eaten cold maize porridge and sour milk all day to read recipes that use meat, grated cheese, fried onions and mashed potato. The closest we ever get to meat is the bright pink, processed meat we call polony and something we call "walkie talkies"—chicken feet cooked in a spicy sauce. Sometimes I go with Potso and other boys in the village to hunt tiny field mice that run along the contour lines of a field and we have a mouse roast on an open fire. But beef mince is never on the menu here.

"Sprinkle with cheese and bake the dish in a moderate oven for forty-five minutes and serve with a green salad..." When I looked up, my grandmother was fast asleep again. I flipped through the magazine, looking for something that didn't wake the hungry dog that lives in my stomach, but it was a very boring magazine. There were pictures of people I didn't know. A sportsman called Hansie Cronje was accused of cheating at cricket; a singer named Britney Spears got arrested for drunk driving. There were pages and pages of the TV guide.

"Hey!" Potso had arrived to see about his phone.

I put my finger to my lips and pointed to my sleeping grandmother. Potso tiptoed and came to sit next to me on the edge of the cardboard in the dust. He knows things are much easier for us if she is asleep.

"Phone not working?" he whispered.

I shook my head.

He sighed. "I'll take it to Mr. Tshezi."

Mr. Tshezi is the man who fixes everything and he lives in the part of the village we call Dark City because it was the last area in Cedarville to get electricity. The darkness never worried Mr. Tshezi: he made his own solar panels from which he still charges his cell phone, operates a drill and runs a couple of light bulbs. He can fix anything: old cars, TVs, false teeth, pots...

"Are you reading?" Potso pulled the magazine towards him. "Hey, horoscopes. Which one are you?"

"Taurus, I think. But this magazine is old."

"That doesn't matter. We'll see if it came true." Potso was determined to read. Here was another person in my life whose name should have been different. I think Stubborn suits him better.

"Okay, Mr. Taurus. While the moon is in the phase of Sagittarius, you can expect major changes in your life. You will travel to distant places. Expect changes in your home environment. Your love life..." Potso stopped to grin at me and jiggled his eyebrows. "Your *love life* will show a marked improvement as many people will be attracted to your zest for life. Your lucky number is 25."

Potso punched me on the arm. "Distant places! It was that trip to Matatiele a few years ago when you had that bad attack of worms. You see, it's all true."

"Except for the bit about my love life. No *marked improvement* there." Potso knows everything about me, even my feelings for Sesi. She is my teacher's daughter, the prettiest girl in the whole village and in the grade above me at school. I've never told Potso I like her, but he says he can tell, because I get really stupid when I'm around her. But I wouldn't know. When she is near, I feel as if there is a swarm of bees in my head, and I can't think straight or remember anything.

"Give her time. Of course she'll love you now that you don't have those terrible worms anymore."

Potso got bored with the horoscopes and went inside to fetch his phone.

And that was when I turned the page and read the story that changed our lives forever.

A RED PAPERCLIP

The title of the story was "Man Trades Paperclip for a House," and I remember thinking that was impossible. Who would swap a paperclip for a house? It was a big house too—there was a photo—two-story wooden house in a town called Kipling in Canada. And there was a photo of Kyle MacDonald, the man who traded the paperclip and ended up with the house. He had a big smile on his face, as you can imagine.

Potso came out of the house carrying the phone and its back cover in two hands. "It's in two pieces," he complained.

"Forget the phone. Listen to this story." And I read it to him aloud.

A year ago Montreal resident Kyle MacDonald advertised a red paperclip on the internet. His plan was to keep trading, each time with something of a higher value until he reached his goal: a house.

"I couldn't afford the down payment on a house," said Kyle MacDonald. "I was feeling depressed and was staring at this red paper clip on my desk when I got my idea. I decided to advertise it on the internet and see if anyone would give me something in exchange for it. I was happy to trade for anything as long as it was of a higher value."

Well, it took him a year, fourteen trades and many trips all over Canada and the USA, but his dream of owning a house has come true. On July 12th of this year, the town of Kipling handed MacDonald the keys to his house.

"Hayi man!" Potso laughed. He wasn't buying it. But I read on.

"My first trade was for a pen that was shaped like a fish. I traded that for a ceramic door handle in Seattle. Someone in Massachusetts had read my blog site and offered to trade me a Coleman stove in exchange for the door handle. I had to travel quite a distance to make these trades—but what did I have to lose?

"I advertised the Coleman stove with the offer of a cooked meal and traded that for a small electric generator. Then someone in New York City offered to trade the generator for a keg of beer and a neon Budweiser sign."

Potso stopped me. "What's a neon Budweiser sign?"

"It must be a Canadian thing, I suppose. Maybe it's like the sign outside the Cedarville shop that says 'Coo-ee—So much yum for everyone.' You don't have to understand everything. Just shut up and listen..."

"By now a lot of people were reading my blog site and were getting excited by the direction I was going in. A guy who was the host of a talk radio show in Montreal gave me a great break when he offered to trade a snowmobile for the keg of beer. He mentioned me on his radio station and that gave me a lot of publicity. Suddenly people wanted to interview me and I made guest appearances on national TV. On one of these appearances, I mentioned as a joke that the only place I would not be prepared to travel to make a trade was a town called Yahk in British Columbia. Well, you can guess what happened. The good citizens of Yahk decided to make an offer on the snowmobile and in exchange, they offered a trip to Yahk, including airfares, meals, and skiing. Someone offered me a supply truck in exchange for the trip. I was then offered a recording contract, which I traded for a year's free rent in Phoenix, Arizona. I traded that for an afternoon with superstar Alice Cooper."

"Alice Cooper can't be much of a superstar if I've never even heard of her," Potso complained.

I ignored him and read on.

"At this point, I made a risky exchange and traded the Alice Cooper experience with a snow globe, which is just an ornament although a rare one. A famous actor in America, Corben Benson, was a collector of these snow globes and he offered me a role in his next movie in exchange for the snow globe. Where I live, a part in a movie is serious currency. This is where the town of Kipling came in on the deal. By now I had *generated a lot of publicity for my quest and the people of Kipling figured that it would help to put their town on the map and attract tourists if they were able to offer me a house in their town. They decided to hold a talent contest in the town for the movie role.*

"And that is the story of how I traded a red paper-clip for a house!"

"So what's a snowmobile or a snow globe?" Potso asked. He'd missed the whole point of the story.

"How must I know? And it doesn't matter!" I wanted to shake him. "It's the idea, Stupid! It's the best idea I've ever heard of!" Excitement was zipping through me like an electric current. I could *feel* it. Why couldn't he?

"This is crazy," said Potso. "But perhaps the people who live in Canada have too many houses and not enough brains. No one would be stupid enough to make that kind of trade here."

"Well, I'm going to try it. I'm going to find something to trade and try and get something of a higher value. Then maybe someone will, you know, give me a new house too."

"In your dreams. Things like this only happen to people who live in Canada. This. Is. Cedarville. People who live in Cedarville don't get given houses for paper-clips. You don't even have a paperclip!"

"I know. But I'll find something, you'll see."

And that was how the whole thing started.

HOUSE

It took some time for my eyes to adjust to the dark of the house, having been in the sunlight outside. Potso followed me inside and started pulling things out, making silly suggestions.

"A tin cup? A ragged blanket? No, no, wait! Ladies and gentlemen, who will give a large house in exchange for this old bucket?"

I ignored him—sometimes Potso could be really annoying—and looked around our house. It's got a door, two windows, and a roof as well as a pit toilet in the garden, but a person needs more than those basics to be comfortable. I knew where to position my mattress so that I didn't get wet when it rained. Those tiny pinpricks of light that shone through the tin were not stars. But when you don't have ceiling boards, it's like living inside a saucepan in the summer and a fridge in the winter. Sometimes the frost in mid-winter is so bad, that toothpaste—when we have it--freezes in the tube if it has been left up against the window. The linoleum floor curled like old bread in the corners and the walls were blackened in places from candle smoke and the paraffin stove. We do have electricity in our house, but it had been years since we could afford to buy the vouchers from the shop so the single fly-spotted light bulb swung uselessly in the breeze in the middle of the room.

Ours is a typical two-room house: you'll see my grandmother's bed, my foam mattress under it, the kitchen and the sink as you walk in the door. My father's bed and a wardrobe is on the other side of the dividing wall. I keep my few clothes in a large zipped bag at the foot of the bed. Only my father and my grandmother use the wardrobe, but I opened it any-way, looking for inspiration.

A stack of bright orange traffic cones fell out and hit me on the head. I knew I couldn't trade one of those. They didn't even belong to my father. They were the property of the local municipality. My father had a job with the Municipal Road Maintenance Project. He broke up chunks of gravel with a pick and cleared storm water drains with a spade. But it was just for that month. The job was rotated so that other people got a chance to earn some money. Most people are un-employed in this village. When the government built all these houses, they forgot to make sure that there were jobs for the people who would live in them. Some peo-ple have work on nearby farms, or they work for the municipality or in one of the few shops in the village. Dad used to have a steady job at the *Kromdraai* cheese factory, but that closed down many years ago. Since then, life has been very hard. Sometimes he gets work on farms helping to milk cows, make silage or harvest turnips, but it's never anything permanent. We are lucky that my grandmother gets her pension from the Social Security office in Matatiele once a month and often, that is all we have to live on.

I stuck one of the traffic cones on my head and looked at my reflection in the shard of mirror that rests on the high window ledge in my father's room. I'm tall for my age, twelve, almost thirteen, so I can see my face easily, but Potso is short and had to jump to see his reflection. He put the bucket on his head and pushed me out of the way to see himself, but the bucket kept falling over his eyes. So he just staggered around with his head in the bucket, banging into the cupboard and falling over the corner of the bed. When he barged into the kitchen, tin plates clattered to the floor and the pap pot fell off the stove.

He was crashing about like this when my grandmother hobbled into the doorway again to see where all the noise was coming from.

"I thought there was a jackal loose in the house, with all this noise! I should have known it would be Piet and Potso. Out you go! Hambani!" As we ran past her in the doorway, she poked us with her walking stick.

Sometimes, when I make an unwelcome noise, my grandmother calls me "Piet" after the bird we call a

Piet-my-Vrou. It's a type of cuckoo that only arrives for the summer and on hot summer nights, it calls all night long and keeps us awake. *Piet-my-vrou! Piet-my-vrou!* My grandmother said that when I was a baby, just as she'd be dropping off to sleep, I'd cry out like this cuckoo. And it drove her crazy.

"Where shall we go? Shop? Soccer field?" Potso asked when we were on the road.

"No," I said, because I'd got an idea. "The river. I know what I'm going to make as my first trade."

Potso laughed and shook his head. He knew what I was planning. "That man in Canada who traded the red paper clip was a bit crazy. But anyone who trades something for one of your clay animals is really mad in the head." He made spirals round his ears with his fingers. "Project paperclip...*heh-heh-heh.*" He laughed.

But he came with me anyway.

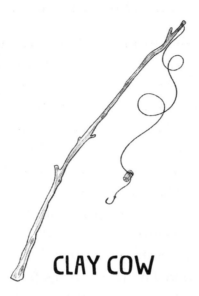

CLAY COW

It is the favorite thing of adults in my village to give children seen walking along a road: jobs to do.

"If you are going to the shop, please buy me paraffin."

"Take this pole quickly to Mrs. Twala at the taxi rank."

"Please take this money to the lady selling turnips outside the post office."

"Hurry! You must be back before my spit dries."

And this time was no different.

"Boipelo! Boi–COUGH."

"Yes, Mkhulu." We stopped outside Mkhul' uGaba's house at the end of our street. Although he is not my grandfather, I still call him Mkhulu because my culture expects me to show this respect to all elders. And any- way, in my village, we all share family members: aunts, uncles, brothers, sisters, parents and grandparents belong to us all.

Mkhul' uGaba spent his days coughing while he sat in an old plastic chair in a patch of sun outside his door. Potso and I often did small jobs for him like collecting amalongwe for his fire. My father told us that the smoke from these dried cow pats was probably bad for his chest, but it's not so easy to find wood; most of the dead trees get chopped up quickly and taken home by the women who carry them in big bundles on their heads. Sometimes Mkhul' uGaba asked us to fill the rusty enamel basin that sits just outside his gate with fresh water for the stray dogs that roam up and down snuffling for food. I do these things for him because I want to help—I too know what it's like to be hungry—but also because he is Sesi's friend. She is often at his house cooking pap for the stray dogs and cats. Once I cleaned the pap-encrusted basin for her, and so I hoped that he would put in a good word for me.

But in spite of all their efforts, the dogs remained as bony as ever. And over the past few months, Mhkul' uGaba had become so thin himself that he looked like a man made of wire that is covered in rags.

I didn't know what was wrong with him in those days, and we didn't talk about it. I knew it was possible that he had tuberculosis, TB. But we only heard about these things at school. Mrs. Dlali, our Life Orientation teacher, was always terrifying us with stories about HIV and AIDS and TB. Apparently if you get TB, you have to go away from home and stay in a clinic for many, many months so people can check you take your medicine. Nobody wants that. And if you have AIDS, everyone will know that you are going to die. Nobody wants that either. So outside of Life Orientation, we just pretended it didn't happen. Mrs. Dlali told us that there are pills you can take to help you live a long life— yet people are dying all the time, so I don't know if they work. All I knew was that I didn't want to think about it or talk about it.

Mkhul' uGaba tried to talk, but a fit of coughing made it impossible. So he summoned us with a hoop of his arm.

"Are you going...to the river?" he asked, breathing heavily, as we stood before him.

We nodded.

"Will you catch me a fish? I'm not hungry—but I must eat. I'll get you my...COUGH, COUGH, COUGH."

Using all his strength, he pushed down on his legs to get up out of the chair, tightened the string that was holding up his trousers and shuffled into his house. He emerged with a hand-made fishing rod—a stick with some fishing line and a hook—and a ball of cold pap for us to use as bait. This dry maize meal porridge feeds all of us: people, stray dogs, fish...

While Potso fished, I squatted on the river bank under a willow tree with a lump of clay, rolling it into a sausage then gently pulling out bits to make the head, the legs and the horns. I even gave it a tiny udder. I sang as I worked.

"If you sing like that, you'll frighten the fish," Potso complained.

I threw a lump of clay at him and took the small clay cow down to the river to smooth its surface with river water. Then I put it carefully to dry in a patch of sun. I went back to the river to wash the pale mustard-colored clay off my hands and legs.

"Are you entering the talent competition? You know the one Mrs. Jafta told us about?" I asked as I picked the clay out from under my fingernails with a sharp little stick. Mrs. Jafta had told us that someone from the Department of Arts and Culture would be coming to Cedarville to judge a talent contest, and it had caused a lot of excitement at school. There were rumors of sponsorship, but no one knew what or how much.

Potso nodded.

"What will you do?"

"What do you mean?"

"A person like you, with no obvious talents?"

"*A-maaaaze-ing Grace, so sweet the sound that made a wretch like meeee...*" he sang.

"Amazing Grace doesn't *make* a wretch like you, idiot. It's supposed to *save* a wretch like you. But only if you get the words right." I wished I could sing like Potso. He is part of a small choir which I'd give anything to be part of because Sesi is in it too. When Sesi sings, it's so perfect that it almost hurts to listen.

I, however, cannot sing. My grandmother once told me that I couldn't carry a tune even if it was in a bucket.

"So is...er...?" I asked.

"Yes, Sesi is doing the solo. There must be something you could do to impress her. Now you have *project paperclip.*" He waggled his head from side to side like he didn't have his head screwed on right. "Think how impressed she'd be if you turn that clay cow into a hou..." Potso's fishing line gave a sharp downward jerk. "Hey! I caught a fish!"

We gutted the small carp and threaded a reed through its gills so that it would be easy to carry and our hands wouldn't stink of fish. On the way home, Potso sang more just to irritate me: *"Through many dangers, toys, and snails, I have alreeeeeady co-o-o-me ..."* I stopped him by explaining my plans which were starting to take shape: I was going to make posters to advertise the trades and put them up somewhere so everyone could see them. And he was going to draw the posters.

Potso actually has three talents: he knows me better than anyone else on earth, he can sing and he can draw. In isiXhosa, we say someone *"has a hand"* if they are skilled at handwork. Potso has a hand for drawing.

He and I have been friends since Grade One when he tilted so far back in his chair that he crashed to the floor and split his head open. The teacher smacked him on his legs for bleeding on his book and told me to take him to the headmaster's office. But once we were outside the classroom, I took off my school shirt, tied it tightly round his head, and we ran like two rabbits out of the school gates and straight to the river. I don't think we even discussed it, we just went. And we've been friends ever since. I can still see the scar on the back of his head, because his hair doesn't grow on that spot. I like seeing that scar. I don't think he even knows it's there, but every time I see it, I feel like I know something about him that other people don't.

We make a funny looking pair. I'm tall and thin, all legs, long arms, and knobbly knees. I have a long neck and a bony face. But Potso is as his name sounds: round as a caste-iron pot, short and strong. His neck is thick and his face is shiny and wide.

As soon as we'd returned the fishing rod to Mkhul' uGaba and handed over the small, muddy fish—and I'd secretly scanned the vicinity for Sesi, and seen no trace of her—we raced home to work on the poster. I ripped out the middle page from a school exercise book and Potso got a ballpoint pen, knelt on the floor with his bottom in the air, and drew a picture of the clay cow.

I gave advice. "Make it a bit thinner. And the horns longer. Why does it have to look like Mrs. Jackson's sausage dog?"

But Potso ignored me. He wrote in capital letters:
ONE CLAY COW TO TRADE
FOR ANYTHING OF VALUE
CONTACT BOIPELO SEKU.

"Shall we add the phone number?" he asked, sitting up on his haunches.

"It will make us look more professional." We both knew that number would never work, but it would look good.

As soon as Potso finished, I whisked the paper away.

Holding the clay cow in one hand and the poster in the other, I made for the door.

"Let's find somewhere to put this up."

Potso got heavily to his feet and followed me, shaking his head.

"What I like about this plan," I said, "is that it's simple."

Potso just laughed at me.

NONSENSE

But when we got to the main road, I realized that I had no idea where to put it. The library? Only boring people go there: old aunties and kids with nothing else to do. A lamppost? The wind will blow it away.

"We need somewhere with a lot of traffic," I said.

"We could try putting it 'online' like that man from Canada," Potso suggested.

"Online? How?" We have a few computers at school that were donated by some people from overseas. Once we each got a turn to go onto the internet after the teacher showed us how to google. I went blank when it was my chance and typed *Cedarville* with one finger to see if we exist on the World Wide Web, as she called it. And we do! But I'd just started reading that we are part of the Alfred Nzo Municipality when the teacher told me it was someone else's turn. If I had the chance now, I'd probably google Kyle MacDonald to see how he's getting on in his house in Canada.

But Potso didn't mean "online" like the World Wide Web. He thought we could just lay the poster on the railway line and hope that a passing train would shred it to pieces. I twisted his ear until he said he was sorry.

"Outside the shop?" he offered.

And I knew it was the right place: opposite the garage and the only place where farmers, children, and all the residents of Cedarville go to buy anything from a loose sweet to a bag of mealie meal.

As we walked to the shop, I had a good look at the houses to see which one I'd choose to live in. Even Potso started pointing out possibilities.

He jerked his thumb in the direction of an old house with a tin roof and a wide veranda. My grandmother had told me that in the olden days, in the time of apartheid, only white people lived in these proper brick houses. Black people had to live in a place she called "the location." The way she said it made it sound very ugly. Nowadays anyone—town councillors, policemen, or anyone with a good job—can live in any house they can afford. It's strange though: no white people live in Khorong Koali Park with us.

Potso and I peered through the fence at the old brick house. There was a huge vegetable garden out back, which seemed full of overgrown onions, bolted spinach, and half bricks.

"So-so," I said and waggled my head, as if I was out shopping and could have any one I wanted. "But maybe something more modern."

"Okay, tell me about your dream house then, Mr. Fussy."

"Three bedrooms with one just for me with a proper bed and a door I can close. Electricity, running water, a flushing toilet inside the house..."

"A room for the TV," added Potso.

"Yes, big enough for a nice, soft lounge suite and one of those huge wall units."

"For the hi-fi."

"A proper electric stove, not a paraffin one that sits on the floor." When you cook on a paraffin stove, everything in your house—clothes, food and blankets—all have the same hot, rough smell. I don't like it.

"Ceiling boards," said Potso.

"Painted walls," I added. "And a garden."

"A nice room for me, so I can stay over when we've finished watching soccer on TV late at night,"

"Sure," I said. And felt a tiny bit uneasy about how this plan was going to work out for Potso. A house was not something I could easily share with him. But I batted the thought away like a fly.

And then my stomach turned itself inside out. Because just as we came up the steps to the shop, Sesi herself walked out the door. The jolt that shot through my body when I saw her could have been a result of the effect she had on me, or it could have been caused by Potso. He never missed a chance to elbow me in the ribs whenever we saw her.

"Molo Boi," she said as she passed us.

We both turned to watch her small straight back and

the perfect shape of her head as she walked away. Sesi Jafta is, as I think I've mentioned, the most beautiful girl in Cedarville. I could hardly look at her. It is like trying to look at the sun. She has close-cropped hair and a small face with kind, calm eyes. But so do lots of girls. Sesi, though, is different. It is as if she is lit by something from inside. If she is around, I sense her, although she never draws attention to herself.

"Why did she only greet you? What's wrong with me?" asked Potso, pretending to clutch his wounded heart.

I'd been so amazed by her presence, I hadn't even noticed. But now that Potso had pointed out that she'd only greeted me, I stood looking after her like a dumb fence post. Potso had to flap the poster in front of my face to get some life back into me.

We needed to get permission from Mrs. Viljoen, the shop owner, to put up the poster on her wall, so we stood in the queue waiting. She was talking to an old lady we call Mam' uZungu in the funny mixture of isiXhosa and English that some white people use. Mrs. Viljoen has lived in this village for as long as I can remember. You'd think she'd be able to speak proper isiXhosa by now, but we can all understand her, so maybe there's no need.

"Mrs. Zungu," she shouted, though Mam' uZungu is not deaf, just very sick and thin. "*Andi funa u niga wena* this Vicks rub. If you are sick, *uyagula you must hamba*, go to the clinic in Matatiele. *Bazoniga* i-treatment."

Mam' uZungu explained quietly that she didn't have enough money for the taxi to get to Matatiele. She rummaged in a pocket in her skirt and pulled out a small empty tin of menthol rub.

"This is what helps me," she said.

Mrs. Viljoen sighed and reached above her head for a new tin. Mam' uZungu fished out the money that she kept close to her heart, paid, and left. It had been many years since there had been a clinic in Cedarville. Most sick people went through to Matatiele on the taxi to the Maluti Clinic, but the taxi fare was forty rands return. Those who could not afford it just had to get better on their own—or not.

Mrs. Viljoen looked at us over the top of her spectacles that hung on a beaded string. "Yes, boys?"

Potso nudged me in the ribs, and I rubbed my foot behind my leg, which I do sometimes when I am nervous.

"We'd like permission to put up this poster on the wall outside. Please." I showed her the poster. She adjusted her glasses and held it away at arm's length to read it. I showed her the small clay cow that was sitting in the palm of my hand.

"I don't understand. What are you hoping to get for that?" she asked.

"I don't know," I said, suddenly feeling like this was the worst idea I'd ever had. "A man in Canada started with a red paperclip and then...someone gave him a house." I took the folded newspaper article out of my pocket to show her. But she barely glanced at it, because the shop was busy. She reached down to a shelf under the till and found a blob of sticky putty.

"Well, it sounds a bit strange to me. But you can put up your poster outside. I'm very busy today. Dana didn't arrive for work again, so I have to do everything myself and I've got no time for nonsense. No nonsense! Is that clear?"

We said together, "Enkosi! Thank you!" And we shot out of the shop, feeling jubilant. So far, so good.

We put up the poster, found a bit of old cardboard to sit on, and leaned back against the shaded wall to escape the afternoon sun. The clay cow sat between us. Potso took the broken phone out of his pocket and looked at it. "You really know how to break a phone." He blew on it to dry out its insides.

Mam' uZungu was leaning against the railing as if she was trying to get the strength to walk down the steps to the pavement. "Is that phone working? I need to phone my daughter," she called.

Potso looked at me accusingly—as if I'd broken his perfectly good phone all by myself—and said, "No, Ma, I'm sorry, it's not working."

She inched her way down the steps, leaning heavily on the railing. She looked like a bent old tree that had been pushed by the wind.

"And now we wait for the people to come running ...for *project paperclip*," said Potso and he laughed. He wiggled his bottom to get comfortable on the cardboard.

It didn't take long. There was a small crowd outside the bottle store, which was just the other side of a small road, facing the shop. These were the young guys who didn't have work. They seemed to spend most of their days hanging about, sharing a single cigarette and looking for anything to relieve the boredom. As soon as I saw them, I knew that trouble was coming. Three of them walked slowly over and looked at the poster.

"And this...is the cow?" asked Luvo and he nudged the clay cow with his foot.

They sucked their lips in to stop themselves from laughing.

"Yes," said Potso. "He wants to swap it for anything that's worth more. This guy in Canada did it with a red paperclip, and he eventually got a house."

That was too much for them, and their sniggering erupted into full belly laughs.

"Well, I'll give you something that has a higher value," said Luvo and he picked up an empty silver pie plate that was lying on the ground near the rubbish bin. He held it out with a look of mock seriousness.

The other two laughed and slapped the wall. Then they all did high fives with each other and walked back across the road. We could see them entertaining the other guys with the story. Soon they were all pointing at us and rolling around on the grass enjoying the joke.

Potso clicked his tongue and stared straight ahead. I hid the clay cow under the pie plate.

Then three of our friends arrived: Jude, Mawili, and Prince. They had come to buy a loose cigarette. Where they'd got the money for that, I don't know. They all stared at the poster.

"We are trading," I said, hoping to explain before the confusion started. "If you bring us something that's worth more than this cow, we'll give you the cow."

"So where's the cow?" asked Mawili.

I pulled it out from under the pie foil.

"And if we give you something, you will give us *that?*" I could tell they didn't think it was such a great deal.

By now, I was really regretting this plan. It had sounded so simple at home but so stupid and complicated now that it was out in public.

But Jude seemed to think it might work.

"Come guys," he said. "Let's play. We'll go and see what we can find."

They all ran off down the street.

About ten minutes later, they were back. They'd brought a whole crowd of kids with them. Some of the younger ones seemed to think I was handing out sweets or something and they stood in front of me, holding out their hands.

Prince pushed them aside.

"Here," he said. "Is this the sort of thing you want?"

He held out an old slip slop that he said he'd found down by the railway line.

"No." I was weary of the whole thing, and we'd not even made the first trade.

"What about this?" someone pushed an old toy car with no wheels under my nose.

"If I give you this, will I get the house?" asked one bright spark who tried to offer me his library book.

Everyone was pushing and shoving and trying to get me to look at the rubbish they had brought. Some of them were even raiding the bin for more garbage. They were all shouting and laughing. One of the little children got pushed and rolled down the bank and hit her head on a stone. Her cries brought Mrs. Viljoen outside with a face like thunder.

"Potso and Boipelo!" she shouted above the noise. "I said I didn't want any nonsense. And this..." she waved her arm at the crowd of children, "is NONSENSE! Everybody must go home. Hambani! Boipelo, you can stay here by yourself."

She disappeared inside the shop.

Everyone went home and left me sitting outside under my stupid poster. Potso turned to wave at me, but I pretended not to see him and stared down the road.

PIE-IN-THE-SKY

There was a bit of traffic that afternoon. A few farmers who came to get the *Kokstad Advertiser* and a liter of milk and some people I knew from Cedarville came to buy green soap and Boxer tobacco. Some of them read my poster and one farmer's wife patted my head as she passed as if I was a pet dog. I suppose Mrs. Viljoen must have told them what I was doing.

To this day, I don't know why I sat there so long. I could have pulled that poster down and run home. But I buried my head in my hands, imagining what a fool I'd look if Sesi came back to the shop and saw me. I tried to think of something I could do at the talent show. If I was going to get Sesi to notice me, I knew I had to have at least some talent. Some boys were going to be doing soccer tricks, tapping a ball with their feet and heads. I'd seen them practicing in the school play-ground. But they'd never include me. I can play soccer, and I like running about screaming LADUUUMA! when someone scores a goal (it's never me), but no one would want to watch me tapping a ball with my foot or doing a header. I'd just make a fool of myself. And I'm all right at dancing. I can shuffle about and keep time, but I'm not one of those kids in the playground who spins on his shoulders or shimmies and shakes like he's made of rubber. I realized there wasn't much I could do. I just wasn't a talented person. I couldn't even get someone to play my stupid trading game.

Then Mrs. Viljoen stuck her head round the corner of the shop. "Come on, Boi! You might as well help me if you're going to sit there all day. I've given up waiting for Dana."

I put the clay cow carefully in my pocket—I didn't want to break the horns—and followed her into the shop. She pointed to a pile of thick slices of white bread and some pink sliced polony on a table behind the till.

"I need you to wrap two slices of bread and two slices of polony in this plastic." She pointed to a roll of thin sticky plastic.

I wrapped about 10 packs very tightly using as little plastic as I could. If Dana wasn't going to return to work, I wondered if Mrs. Viljoen would give me her job. I could do it after school and I imagined all the money I could earn. I swept the floor of the storeroom, although she didn't ask me to do it, just to prove to her how well I could work.

Through the storeroom door, I spotted Aunty Shirley from the library. She'd come in to buy a packet of Marie biscuits and a magazine. Mrs. Viljoen was talking about me in a hushed voice, but I could hear what they said.

"Well, at least he's *doing* something. As I said to Meneer Venter when he came to get his newspaper, I said, 'Meneer Venter, it might be a bit pie-in-the-sky, but at least someone in this godforsaken village is actually *doing* something.'"

"Ja, I suppose you right, hey," said Aunty Shirley. "You know what I think? The biggest problem in this place might not be unemployment. I think it's *laziness*. People just need to get off their *backsides* and do something. It's no good sitting around and waiting for the *government...*"

"Ha! The government." I heard the clang of the till open.

I hung the broom on the back of the store room door and went back into the shop. Mrs. Viljoen and Aunty Shirley stopped talking. Maybe they thought I'd be offended if they didn't like the government. I didn't care about the government—but I did care that they thought all poor people were just lazy. They obviously didn't know our neighbor Sis' uNomazizi who got up at 5 a.m. to cook and do her family's washing before catching a taxi at 6:30 to her job in Matatiele. She had to leave her little baby girl at the daycare behind the Methodist church. I once heard her telling my grandmother that she didn't like doing that because she worried that the baby just got left to lie in her cot for hours and she thought that sometimes they smacked her if she cried. She showed us the bruises on her little leg. I knew that Sis' uNomazizi could not work harder than she was doing. But her life never improved. My own father used to walk ten kilometers to get to a farm in the Mvenyane when there was seasonal work reaping mealies and ten kilometers back in the evening.

I didn't know what the problem was, but I did know it wasn't laziness.

"Family well otherwise?" asked Mrs. Viljoen.

"Ja, no complaints, hey," Aunty Shirley replied.

I wiped the big fridge with care, imagining while I did so the fridge that we would one day have in our new house. I replaced the three packets of Rama margarine and two pieces of fried chicken that took up a whole shelf.

"Thank you, Boi. You can stock the fridge with these cool drinks now," said Mrs. Viljoen. She pointed to a pile of crates with two-liter Cokes and some cardboard boxes of cold drink cans piled up against the wall. I lined all the drinks up in tidy rows in the fridge, making sure that they all faced the same direction.

"Well, you've done a good job," said Mrs. Viljoen as she peered over her glasses at me.

She paused and then she said: "Now bring me that clay cow. I'll trade you a two-liter Coke for it."

I fished in my pocket, brought out the clay cow, its surface already dry and powdery. She took out a blob of sticky putty, put a piece carefully under each leg and stuck it firmly on top of the till.

I could not believe it. I'd just made my first trade! It

wasn't at all what I'd expected but a two-liter bottle of Coke was certainly worth more than a lump of river clay. Mrs. Viljoen jerked her head in the direction of the fridge as if to say, "Go on. Take it."

I took a Coke out of the fridge, said, "Thank you, Mrs. Viljoen," and left the shop.

As soon as I got outside, I punched the air with my fist and ran as fast as I could to Potso's house.

THE HOLE IN THE BUCKET

Potso lives at number 557 in a gray block house that is identical to ours except his house had a white van parked outside on bricks, piles of old tin and barbed wire and no peach tree. Potso's mother always had a plan to try and make money, but none of her ideas worked. I could see all the projects she'd tried and abandoned because bits of them lay all over their yard: an abandoned chicken hok—the chickens got eaten by a legavaan lizard; a block mold for a concrete brick-making business—people stole the bricks and she couldn't afford a security guard. She even tried to get tourists from overseas to stay in her house for a "Real South African Experience"—but no one, apart from the one girl from London who thought she was staying in "Khorong Ko-arli Park," wanted a "Real South African Experience" in Cedarville if it meant using a pit toilet outside and the chance to bathe in a plastic bucket with a cup and a face cloth. Her latest project was to restore a white van and sell it back to the garage. From the gate where I stood, I could see her legs in their blue overalls sticking out from under the van.

"Ma!" I called. She pushed herself out from under the van and leaned on one elbow, squinting at me.

"Potso's not here," she said. "He's taken his phone to uMalume uTshezi." And she disappeared back under the van.

So I ran to Mr. Tshezi's place on the other side of the village in Dark City. Sometimes it feels as if my whole day is spent running. It's partly to save time but also, I've noticed that if you run, grown-ups are less likely to give you a job to do: they assume you are already occupied. So I run to school. I run home. I run to Potso's house. I run to the river. It's no wonder I'm always hungry.

I met Potso strolling on the main road on his way home.

"It worked! I got a Coke!" I shouted.

Potso laughed and high-fived me. "Shall we drink it now or later?"

"Are you always this stupid?" I asked him. "Or is today a special occasion?" He lunged for the Coke. I tried to get him in an arm-lock but we both landed up on the grass wrestling for it. Potso is stronger than I am, so he won and pretended to unscrew the lid and take a big gulp.

"OK," he said when the joke had worn off. "Let's go. Project paperclip is up and running. A two-liter Coke to-trade-for-anything-of-a-higher-value."

When we got to my house, we found my father there sitting on the front step, unlacing his boots. His spade was leaning against the house. My grandmother was awake and taking the dry washing off the fence.

"What have you got there?" asked my father, wiping his face with the flat of his hand.

"From Mama uViljoen at the café." I told him the whole story.

He was silent for a long time. He doesn't talk much.

"Well," he said at last. "You won't get a house. You know that? Show me the magazine."

I handed him the page that I'd torn out and he read it aloud so that my grandmother could hear it as well.

"I don't understand," she said. "How did he get the paper clip inside the internet in the first place?"

I left Potso to explain how the internet works while I went inside to get another piece of paper and the ball point pen. From inside the house, I could hear my grandmother's disbelieving voice:

"And someone gave him a *house*? For a paperclip? Is this how they do business in Canada? Well, I suppose it happens here too. You know Constable Mlingisi? He got *three* of those new houses when they were built in Dark City. He didn't give the contractor a paperclip though. I think it had more to do with some lost paperwork that the contractor didn't want anyone to see."

My father sighed. "Ewe. It happens. If you have money or influence. But mostly, things don't work out. Most people's lives are just like leaky buckets that never fill up. You'll spend your whole life pouring in water that just drains away. So don't hope for too much. You will be disappointed."

Potso and I looked at each other and Potso made his *I-told-you-so* face at me. But he took the paper and pen and sat on the step and drew a Coke bottle. He put more detail in than he needed to. He copied the logo perfectly and even wrote ORIGINAL TASTE SINCE 1886, which I'd never even noticed on a Coke bottle before. He added the phone number too, just to make it look professional, as we'd agreed.

I sat beside him but made no comments and gave no advice this time. The excitement I'd felt earlier was leaking out of me—as if I was a holey bucket myself. In truth, I was beginning to think maybe this was a silly dream. Maybe I'd got lucky with the Coke but it was unlikely that this dream would go any further. Everyone I spoke to seemed to think it was a joke, pie-in-the sky. The grown-ups all thought it was a game made up by a child who didn't know how the world really works. Potso looked up at me a few times while he drew, as if he was watching me. Perhaps he sensed my disappointment as the magic just drained away.

"Let's put this up at the soccer match tomorrow afternoon," he suggested. "The Under 15s are playing against Kwabashe. There will be people there who will want the Coke."

It was the fact that he *didn't* make a joke of it that made me feel sad.

When Potso left to go to choir practice at our teacher Mrs. Jafta's house, I sat on the step holding the new poster and watching the shadows lengthen. My father sat in the chair under the peach tree, staring at the street, waiting for something to happen. But nothing did.

Sounds of drunken singing drifted from the shebeen on the corner that sold cheap, home-brewed sorghum beer. Sis' uNomazizi's baby was crying next door. She sang *thula thu thula mntanam, thula sana*...but her voice was tired. Someone coughed. A dog barked.

As soon as the sun goes down, the air gets freezing cold. I pulled on the big padded jacket my father bought from the woman who sells jackets all spread out on the pavement outside the post office. A woman came past, balancing a bucket of water on her head—and the water slopped over the side, wetting her shoulders and her back.

I thought about what my father had said about life being like a leaky bucket. His whole life was spent looking for small, badly paid, temporary jobs. Sometimes there were permanent jobs advertised in the *Kokstad Advertiser*, but those jobs always remained out of reach for him. Once he heard that a garage in Matatiele was offering on-the-job-training for mechanics, but he could not afford to take time off time from his temporary job as a farm worker to get there. Another time, the Farmer's Co-op advertised for a driver, but he didn't have the money to get driving lessons.

It was like that weird song that Mrs. Jafta taught us once hoping we'd learn some English. It was called "There's a hole in my bucket, dear Liza." This man called Henry had a hole in his bucket and his wife Liza gave him lots of ideas about how to fix it—but he needed a bucket of water to wet the stone, to sharpen the knife, to cut the straw, to fix the bucket—and he couldn't do any of it because his bucket had a hole in it. We thought it was a silly song because only an idiot would try to fix a hole in a bucket with straw.

But Mrs. Jafta told us it was supposed to be funny and we were being too serious. That evening as I sat on the step, though, I thought that perhaps it was Mrs. Jafta who hadn't understood the song: if you are poor and your bucket leaks, it doesn't matter how hard you work. Your bucket will never get fixed. Without a bucket to fix your bucket, you just go round in circles.

I crumpled up the poster for the two-liter Coke. You don't fix a leaky bucket with dreams and silly games either.

A DEAL

But the next day Potso arrived back at my house, fished the crumpled poster out of the rubbish bin, rolled it up, and whacked me on the side of my head with it. He insisted that he was going to the soccer game to trade—alone, if necessary. So I picked up the Coke and went.

There was a small herd of bony cows on the field that day—as well as the two donkeys that seem to live there permanently and have to be shooed off the field just before the game starts. And then there were the more regular spectators: a bunch of kids who came to watch or who hoped that one day they'd be able to play for Cedarville Under 15.

There had been a coach for us youngsters once, but he left to go and live in Mount Ayliff and Coach Nontso, who took the Under 15s, tried training us and then gave up. I think it had something to do with Prince and Mawili, who always tackled each other if one of them got the ball—even if they were on the same team. Once, to prevent Prince from getting the ball, Mawili kicked it right over the fence and into the road where it was flattened by a passing taxi. Coach Nontso said that we didn't listen, we tackled our own team mates, we spent more time doing fancy footwork than passing—and he had better things to do with his time.

So we got up to other mischief. Behind the soccer field was the old abandoned cheese factory where my father used to work before it closed down. Someone had cut a hole in the fence and we used to go there to sniff around. We weren't the only ones. We'd see signs that older kids had been there too—those from our school who'd finished matric and couldn't find work, if the graffiti they wrote on the walls was anything to go by. Over time the windows got broken and things disappeared: door handles, taps, water pipes, light fittings, linoleum. Years ago, the place was tidy and everything worked, but now the building looked like a shaggy old monster: from the soccer field, I could see the fangs of broken glass in the old windows.

The old factory belonged to Mr. Retief who also owned the farmer's co-op next to the cheese factory. He had a bad temper. Once he had caught some of us in the old cold storage room. He said that if he ever caught us there again, he would shut us in there for the weekend. So I kept away from the place, but Prince, Jude, and Mawili liked to go there, especially on match days, looking for trouble. In fact, when we arrived at the field, those three were nowhere to be seen.

The soccer players were at the far end of the field doing warm up exercises.

The team from Kwabashe had not arrived yet, so the atmosphere was still peaceful. Someone had a bucket of soil and was filling in the holes on the field and trying to flatten the lumps with a spade. Someone else was marking wobbly lines with lime that came out of a funny old tin on wheels.

The Kwabashe team are tough and play dirty. But matches are always entertaining, mostly because they give us spectators lots to complain about: the ref is always wrong, there are always unseen fouls that we like to bring to his attention, and we all know that we can do better than the players on the field. If the Cedarville team loses, it is always because the game was rigged, and we are united in our outrage. If we win, it's because we earned it and we are beside ourselves with joy.

Anyway, Potso and I found a place on the fence where there was a bit of wire sticking out and impaled our rumpled poster on it, sat on the grass, and waited. I just hoped that a Coke would be less ridiculous than a clay cow.

Some people were heading in our direction. My heart jumped into my throat and tried to claw its way out through my mouth. I busied myself by moving the Coke into the shade of the fence post and flattening an area of grass so that the bottle didn't topple over.

There were four of them. Potso nudged me and spoke out of the corner of his mouth as they came closer.

"It's Sesi and her friends."

What was wrong with me? Whenever I saw her, my insides turned to water. I didn't know if I wanted her to notice me or ignore me, if I wanted to be in her company or far away from her. I wanted to talk to her, but I dreaded opening my mouth because, when I did, only garbled nonsense came out. I picked at the grass. My heart was hammering.

"Hi Boi. Hi Potso. So what's the story with the Coke?" she asked. "Are you selling it?"

I nudged Potso to do the talking. He nudged me back. It couldn't carry on like this: one of us had to talk, so I opened my mouth and hoped that understandable words would come out of it.

"No...I am wanting to trade...um...swap stuff. You see there's this guy in Canada actually in a sort of magazine and he did this thing with a red paperclip on the internet and he traded it for...um...stuff and each time he traded, he made sure that it was something with a higher value and then he...um...he got a house." I gabbled like the turkey that I was.

"Sorry, what?" said Sesi, and she tilted her head to one side.

The other girls started to giggle. Potso came to my rescue.

"He just wants to trade the Coke for something. Anything. He doesn't want money for it."

I don't know if that made any more sense to them than my explanation but Sesi said, "I hope it works out. Good luck."

Some people could say those exact same words and make it sound mean, but she said it in a really nice way— like she meant it. When she walked off with her friends, Potso and I stared after them.

"Close your mouth," said Potso. "You look even more stupid with your mouth hanging open like that."

I snapped my mouth shut and boxed him hard on the shoulder. We wrestled about in the grass, trying to hit one another.

"So which one of you has got this Coke I keep hearing about?" asked a voice from someone towering over us. We sat upright quickly. It was Chipo the goalie from the Under 15s soccer team.

"Um...that's me!" I said. "Have you got something you want to trade?"

"Nothing," he opened his hands. "I've pulled my hamstring so I can't even play soccer. Coach is looking for a new goalie." We clicked our tongues sympathetically.

"Hayi, I think today's game's been canceled anyway. Kwabashe haven't arrived. If they don't move it, they are going to have to concede."

"You guys are at the top of the table," said Potso.

Chipo nodded and looked off into the distance where a group of boys were practicing nifty tricks with a soccer ball. Some of them could roll the ball onto their back and tap it to each other without letting the ball touch the ground.

"They are pretty good," said Chipo. "I think they are practicing for the talent show..." He suddenly snapped his fingers. "Don't give that Coke to anyone. I'm just going to speak to Coach and I'll be back. I might have something to trade with you."

"Okay," I replied, trying to sound very casual. "But you'll have to get back to us quickly because other people have also made us offers."

He went off, limping, to find the coach, and I glanced at Potso who was looking at me as if I had just swindled my own grandmother out of her pension money. I said: "And you can close your mouth. You also look stupid with it hanging open."

Potso laughed and gave me another of his flat-handed clips across the head. I would have punched him back but we heard a commotion behind us. Someone over at the old cheese factory was yelling...

Mr. Retief had caught our friends Jude, Mawili, and Prince! He bellowed at them as they all tried to wriggle through the small hole in the fence together. "Bugger off! The lot of you!" he shouted.

We laughed when Mr. Retief's shoe almost nicked Jude's backside just as he managed to squirm under the fence. Potso flicked his fingers to make the cracking sound of a whip: *"Yoh, yoh, yoh!"* We do that when people are in trouble.

But behind Mr. Retief, we could see our other friend Aviwe darting between buildings of the old factory, trying to hide himself. Aviwe can't run as fast as the rest of us: his one leg is a bit thinner than the other and his foot is a funny shape. Mr. Retief turned away from the fence and spotted him. Potso sucked air through his teeth. We both held our breath.

Mr. Retief could have caught him, but he walked off back towards the Farmer's Co-op flicking his hand above his head as if to say Voetsek! Aviwe took his chance and ran hobbeldy-hop, hobbeldy-hop towards the hole in the fence. He can move surprisingly fast when he has to. We all cheered as he wriggled to safety. Then all four walked over to us, laughing, and flopped down in the grass.

"Eish! That was close," said Jude. "Did you see how he kicked me?" He swiveled round to examine the injury to his backside.

"Aaagh, he hardly touched you," said Potso, who could always be relied upon to tell the truth.

Mawili checked the time on his phone: "Half an hour late. It looks as if the Kwabashe team isn't going to arrive."

"They're scared of us," said Aviwe. "Ai! Here comes Coach. He's going to ask you to be a linesman, Mawili."

Mawili sat up, alarmed. Coach dropped to his haunches to talk to us. Chipo remained standing, rubbing the back of his thigh.

"We want to make you a deal," said Coach.

It was a complicated trade. Coach Nontso only agreed to it because the Cedarville team was at the top of the league and, because the Kwabashe team taxi had broken down on their way to Cedarville, the match would have to be conceded, which made their position even more secure.

It turned out that, because of Chipo's hamstring

injury, he needed to rest for a few weeks. But if we were willing to give Chipo the Coke, Coach was happy to give a younger player a chance in next week's game against the Kokstad Under 15s. He was hoping to find some new talent for the team and he needed a goalie reserve anyway.

"I'll leave it to you two and Chipo to find the replacement," said Coach Nontso, pointing with his finger at the three of us. "Though I reserve the right to make the final decision. It can be anyone between the age of 13 and 15. And it cannot be either of you." He jutted his chin at Prince and Mawili. "I haven't got the patience to deal with you two magintsas." It seemed a bit unfair. Prince and Mawili might not know who to tackle, but it didn't make them gangsters.

And I wasn't sure about the trade. I worried that a position in a soccer team wasn't a real "thing"—just an opportunity. Then I remembered that once Kyle MacDonald offered someone a chance to act in a movie, which was a similar sort of trade.

A small crowd had gathered to see what was happening, Sesi among them. As soon as I spotted her, I couldn't think straight. What would she want me to do? Potso, at least, seemed clear. He nodded at me, and I decided to just go along with it.

"Do we have a deal?' Coach was getting impatient.

"We have a deal," I said and handed Chipo the Coke. Everyone applauded.

Chipo offered to share it with Coach Nontso, but he didn't want it. All he wanted was a reasonable goalie.

Chipo unscrewed the top slowly and took a big, long drink. A few of the girls gave a cheer and clapped as he wiped his mouth with the back of his hand. Some of the little boys jumped up at him, begging for a sip, but he swatted them off with his free hand.

"Come, Sesi," he said. "I'll share it with you."

The rest of the soccer team whooped and hit Chipo on the back. But Sesi just smiled and shook her head. Other girls would have done anything for Chipo's attention, but I knew Sesi wouldn't do it. I swallowed with relief when she said no. I had thought, though, that I was the only one who noticed her—the fact that she'd obviously caught Chipo's eye made me uneasy.

But the trade was a good one, I realized. On the way home from the soccer field, we had about twelve offers for the place in the team. Every boy between the ages of about six and fourteen wanted a chance to play goalie in the next match. The risk was that they would have nothing valuable to trade. Some of them took off their dirty T-shirts as we walked and tried to give them to me.

"We will only consider serious offers," shouted Potso above the noise. "We'll be outside the shop tomorrow morning. You can bring your stuff there."

"And don't bring rubbish!" I added. "No library books, stolen things or dirty T-shirts!" I was starting to feel more confident about this whole trading thing.

AMAZING GRACE

That evening, I went with Potso to his choir rehearsal at Mrs. Jafta's house which is in Dark City. Because it's where Sesi lives too, I felt like there was an invisible string that came from that house that was wrapped around my heart wherever I went.

Anyway, I had nothing better to do that evening and it gave me a chance to see Sesi, even though I still didn't trust myself to talk to her.

We arrived late. The other five members of the choir were already there, Sesi too of course. They all squashed into Mrs. Jafta's lounge. She'd pushed the couch and chairs against the wall and stood in the doorway of the kitchen to conduct them. I stood outside in the garden, looking through the window.

"Now I don't want anyone singing this hymn like they are bored," Mrs. Jafta scolded the choir. "I know you've all heard it a million times. But it's about something important. Perhaps one of the great mysteries of life. What is it about?" She glared at Potso—maybe because he was the last to arrive.

"Amazing grace?" he said nervously.

"Yes, amazing grace. And why is grace so amazing? Tell us, Potso."

"Because you're saying thanks for the food?"

"No, grace is not only about saying thanks for the food. Although that is one of its meanings. In this hymn, grace is a gift. What kind of gift?"

Potso just scratched his head and looked at the floor. Gifts were not a regular thing where we lived.

Mrs. Jafta tried again. "If you get a gift for your birthday, is that the same as grace?"

Sesi shook her head. "I don't think it's something you buy. It's more like a kind of blessing."

Mrs. Jafta pressed on, wanting to squeeze the word for every possible meaning. "Yes, and what do you feel when you get the gift or the blessing of grace?"

"Pleased?" Potso was still trying to get the right answer.

"When you are lost and then you are found, like it says in the song, you feel a lot more than pleased."

"Relieved," someone else said. "It's like you think nothing is going to work out...and then it does. And everything is OK."

"Yes!" at last Mrs. Jafta had the answer she was looking for. "You feel sweet, sweet relief if you are lost, and then you are found. When something feels impossible and then it comes right and it is wonderful, grace is like that."

Everyone nodded.

"It happens suddenly and unexpectedly, but you'll know it when it comes to you. It takes place in lots of different ways, but it always happens at just the right time: sometimes it is dark and suddenly there's some light to see by. Or it's the gift of a looking at something that is all knotted and impossible to undo. And you look and you look—but you can't see how to undo it. Then maybe there's this *click*..." She snapped her fingers. "And you see that if you just loosen this or pull that, the knot will untangle. So I want you to sing like it's the amazing gift that it is."

The sermon over, Mrs. Jafta beat time on the door post. "Five, six, seven, eight..."

The Choir sang without musical accompaniment.

"Amaziiiing Grace, how sweet the sound..."

Sesi's voice soared over the harmonies. The sound reminded me of a bird in flight, like a swallow at dusk dipping its beak in the river to drink.

In the darkness, I heard a cough and turned to see Mkhul' uGaba standing under the peach tree, holding onto the trunk with one hand and conducting the choir with the other, with his eyes closed. If anyone needed this grace that Mrs. Jafta was talking about, it was him. Why didn't he get any of this unexpected magic?

I could remember the time when he was the best singer in church. His deep voice could cut a path through mountains and wherever he went, we followed: if he started a hymn we all joined in. If he repeated lines, we all repeated them.

Since he got sick, Mrs. Jafta had taken over leading the hymns. But I knew that every Saturday evening, he ate supper with Mrs. Jafta and Sesi, to discuss the hymns for church the next day. I knew this because every Saturday evening, I looked out for Sesi walking him slowly home after supper with her arm looped through his.

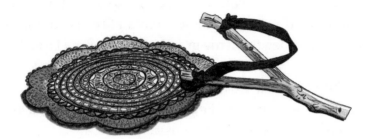

ONCE-IN-A-LIFE-TIME OPPORTUNITY

The next morning, although I was longing to get to the shop and see what could be traded for the place in the Cedarville soccer team, I first had to go to church with my grandmother. The hours dragged: there was some singing, a lot of praying, some reading from the Bible. The voice of the priest droned on and on in that old-fashioned English that makes everything sound dark and difficult.

Then I looked on all the works that my hands had done. And on the labor in which I had toiled; and indeed all was vanity and grasping for the wind. There was no profit under the sun.

"All is vanity and grasping for the wind," repeated the priest just in case we hadn't heard the miserable message the first time. I glanced down at the large watch that my grandmother wears on her wrist. It was quarter past nine. About an hour later, I glanced again and it was twenty minutes past nine. I twisted round to make eye contact with Potso, who was sitting with his mother at the back of the church and received only a pinch on my leg from my grandmother for my trouble.

Then I had to walk my grandmother home. At the intersections, she just kept walking. I thought maybe she couldn't see the road signs.

"There's a stop street here," I told her.

"Yes," she said. "And it's a good thing too because some people drive very badly."

So by the time I got to the shop, there was already a small crowd. Potso had put up the poster, which read, "Once-in-a-lifetime opportunity to play goalie for the Cedarville Under 15s. All offers to Boipelo Seku or Potso Sebetso." He and Chipo were trying to organize everyone.

"I thought you weren't coming," said Potso.

I shrugged. "My grandmother walks slowly."

"I'm here to do quality control," said Chipo. "So you, you, and you—hambani!" He flapped his hand at Prince and Mawili and a tiny boy who looked about six years old, telling them to go.

"Everyone, put your things against the wall!" bossed Potso. "Boi and I will look at them." Everyone surged towards the wall. "And don't bother putting anything down if you can't play soccer!"

There was a scramble, then everyone stood back— and Potso, Chipo, and I walked along the wall to see what we had to choose from.

It was a sad selection: a home-made catapult, a tennis ball, a bar of used soap with deep cracks, a large floppy crocheted doily, a framed picture of roses with a Bible verse—and then, as if to remind me *again* of how pointless the whole thing was—a red bucket with a broken handle.

Potso walked up and down with his hands behind his back, shaking his head and clicking his tongue as if he was a headmaster disappointed in the day's homework results. There really was nothing of value in this line that was worth the trade.

Suddenly there was the sound of a deep base beat, *DOEM chukka, DOEM chukka*, and the roar of an engine. Malume uVezi, Aviwe's dad, pulled his taxi up outside the café. He hopped out, leaving the engine running and the music belting. Aviwe was in the front seat giving passengers their change, with his damaged leg sticking straight out of the taxi.

Malume uVezi took the stairs to the shop two at a time. "Boipelo!" he called. Potso shoved me forward.

"Yes, uncle."

"I've come to make a trade with you. I will give you a week's worth of free transport through to Kokstad if you give my son..." he pointed with his thumb in the direction of Aviwe, "a chance to play in the soccer match."

I must have looked surprised, because he said, "Take your time. Discuss it with Chipo." He turned his back on us while Potso, Chipo, and I talked in low voices.

"A week's worth of free transport is worth...what?"

"About two hundred rand," said Potso.

"But *Aviwe*? Do you think he'll be okay?" Chipo sounded skeptical.

"Can't you give him some training?" I asked.

"I can, but really there's nothing I can do about that leg of his. I mean, *come on,* he can't even run."

"Just think about it, you guys." Potso was exasperated with us. "The position is for a goalie, not a striker. He has to stand in the goals and move this way, and that way." He lunged to the left and the right with his arms above his head. "Aviwe has a good eye for the ball. He will be a hundred percent focused because he can't run like us. A hundred percent."

We both looked at him in silence.

"It's either two hundred rands worth of free transport or this..." Potso kicked the sad old bucket with his toe and it fell over.

"Ok," said Chipo with his hands up as if he was surrendering. "But you two must go and get permission from Coach first."

I nodded at Potso then I went to Aviwe's father and asked him to please wait while we went to ask the coach's permission. The crowd of kids picked up their stuff and went home, sadly carrying their bald tennis balls and crocheted doilies. Potso and I ran up to the Apostolic church to find Coach Nontso. Luckily, he was still there when we arrived, out of breath and panting, so we told him about the offer and about Aviwe.

"I know that boy," he said and he stroked his big

chin, deep in thought.

"He's got a good eye for the ball, Coach. We'll make sure he gets lots of practice. And Chipo will…"

But Coach didn't want to hear more. He clasped both hands together decisively: "OK, boys, you have a deal. Sometimes you find talent in unexpected places, and I'm willing to give this a try. One game only. Just make sure he practices."

He chuckled and shook his head as if he could hardly believe his own stupidity.

FREE TRANSPORT

Word about the free transport traveled almost as fast as Aviwe's father's taxi speeding across the Cedarville Flats in a cloud of dust. The sun wasn't even up. I was still curled up in my blanket on my sponge mattress when there was a loud knock on the door. My grandmother sat up in bed and put her hands to her gray hair. She didn't want anyone to see her without her doek so early in the morning. I handed her the scarf that had fallen on the floor. She tied it round her head quickly before my father could even open the padlock that keeps our door locked at night. I peered around him.

"Yes, Jimmy," said my father. "How can I help you... at..." He rubbed his face with the flat of his hand and looked at his watch "...five o'clock in the morning."

Jimmy Klaasens lives in Dark City. We all knew that he'd once spent time in jail in Matatiele for stealing a farmer's sheep.

"I hear you are giving away free transport to Kokstad." Jimmy Klaasens tightened his ragged jacket around him against the icy early morning wind.

"No," said my father.

"But everyone told me..."

"They told you wrong, Jimmy. I'm not giving anything away for free. But my son here is willing to trade a week's worth of free transport to Kokstad if you give him something in exchange. Have you got something to trade?"

"I might. I might not," said Jimmy Klaasens and he looked up and down the street.

"It's too early to be standing here in the cold wind talking riddles with you. Goodbye." And my father started closing the door.

"No, no, no. Let me show you..." Jimmy Klaasens fished in his jacket pocket and cupped his other hand protectively around something. I caught a glimpse of a gold watch. I whistled through my teeth and looked up at my father.

"Not interested," said my father firmly and shut the door.

"But..." I started.

My father was in no mood to negotiate. "Jimmy Klaasens is a shady character. That watch is almost certainly stolen or fake. He is also a drunk who has been banned from the bottle store here because they refuse to give him any more credit. He probably wants to go through to Kokstad to buy drink."

He plonked the tin kettle down hard on the paraffin

stove to start boiling the water for tea. "You do not want to be trading with men like him."

But before the water even boiled, there was another knock on the door. It was Mam' u-Eugenia from down the road. She was clutching a big plastic zip bag with what looked like a mauve nylon duvet bed-set inside. But before she could even open her mouth, my father said, "No thank you—not interested."

And he closed the door again. Again, I looked at him in astonishment.

"Do you know why Mam' u-Eugenia wants free transport to Kokstad, Boi?" I shook my head. "Well, you don't want to know. But I know and I don't like it. This trading scheme of yours is becoming more trouble than it's worth."

At school it got even worse. It was the end of our Life Orientation lesson, just before break time, and Mrs. Dlali, our teacher, had to shout above the noise: "Everyone who wants to enter the talent competition this Friday must bring their application forms tomorrow! No forms, no entry! Boipelo Seku, please stay behind. I want to talk to you."

I stood reluctantly at her desk while she cleaned the chalk board and packed her bag of books, as if she was stalling for time, waiting for the last person to leave the classroom. Potso hung about the corridor, jumping up like a big puppy to see me through the window. Every time he jumped, he pulled a face. I turned my back on him so I wouldn't laugh. Mrs. Dlali went to close the door.

"Boipelo, I hear that you have a week's worth of free transport through to Kokstad in exchange for something. Is this true?"

"Yes, Mrs. Dlali."

She pulled the marks book out from her large handbag and paged through it, looking sorrowful and shaking her head.

"I see that your marks so far this year for Life Orientation have been very poor. I was wondering if we couldn't come to some understanding. I mean, if you give me something, I could help you. We'd both..."

Sometimes you just open your mouth and a lie just comes out: "I think my father has already organized the trade," I gabbled. "I'm not sure who it's with, but I think it's been done already."

Mrs. Dlali sniffed, closed her marks book, and said I was excused.

I found Potso sitting in the corridor with his back to the wall. "No sitting in the corridors," said Mrs. Dlali as she came past with her nose in the air.

"These grown-ups wanting the transport are so complicated," I complained as soon as she was out of ear shot. "I think she's just offered to improve my LO marks if I give *her* the transport!"

"You should have taken it," said Potso. "Can you imagine the poster? To trade for anything of value: Bopelo Seku's Life Orientation test results. They might have been really popular."

He ducked before I could punch him.

We found Aviwe in the playground and marked off

an area for goalie practice. While Potso stuffed his school jersey into a packet that he found blown against the fence to make a ball we could use, I noticed how busy the playground was. The soccer players were getting better and their tricks niftier. Another group were singing and clapping while some girls who'd tucked their skirts into their pants were dancing so hard, they made the dust fly. Two boys were stick fighting. There were also drum majorettes practicing by the gate. Their leader kept throwing a stick in the air and dropping it. She dropped that stick so many times, it became painful to watch.

Looking at all this talent and effort made me sure that I should not even think about competing. I decided to just sit quietly in the audience and not make a fool of myself. I would put my energy into training Aviwe for the game.

The "ball" was a problem, but we threw it at him over and over and Aviwe dived left and right and caught most of them. He was getting better and Potso was right: he was very focused.

I was tired when I got home from school and the plastic packet in which I carried my books was cutting into my fingers. As I swung open the gate, I saw Sis' uDana, who works for Mrs. Viljoen at the café, sitting on our front step, her one hand resting on a rusty old wheelbarrow.

Before she'd even told me her story, I knew that I would give her the free transport. The wheelbarrow was not a great trade but I knew I'd done the right thing when she said, "Thanks Boi," very softly with tears in her eyes.

I just wanted to be rid of this trade and move on.

PILE OF JUNK

Potso found me washing my school shirt and socks in a plastic basin out under the peach tree.

"Boi!" he shouted from the gate. "I've got something! Refentse says she'll give us a free hair braiding and a hair treatment for the transport. It's worth about three hundred and fifty rand. Good, hey?"

I just stared at him.

"No! No! No! You've gone and done some stupid trade without telling me. I just know you have." I've often wondered how Potso knows what I've done or what I'm going to do—sometimes before I even know myself. "What did you trade?"

I nodded at the wheelbarrow. Potso's mouth fell open. "That pile of junk? Are you crazy?" He clicked his tongue to express his contempt. "Nxa!"

"Don't nxa me!" I was cross. "Dana hasn't been able to go to work because her little daughter Myra is sick in the hospital and she cries for her mother every day. She's got a rash and a fever. Dana really needs that free transport!"

"Haibo! You are not a *social* worker! You'll never get this house if you go round feeling *sorry* for people all the time. You have to make the best trade—FOR A HIGHER VALUE—in case you've forgotten."

"I haven't forgotten."

"But you can't just do stuff without me!"

"I can! This wasn't *your* plan to start with. It was *my* plan. I'm the one who came up with the idea. I can do whatever the hell I want!"

"Ja, except you're all talk and no trousers." Potso got that stubborn look on his face that I have come to know so well. "Fine. If you don't want my help anymore, I'm out. Project paperclip—ha!" He waved his hand like he was swatting away a fly. "And good luck with trading this pile of rubbish, Mr. Social Worker."

He kicked the wheelbarrow once again and marched off down the road.

All afternoon, I hoped that Potso would come back and swat me across the head with the flat of his hand—which is his way of saying sorry—and then I could punch him back to show that I was sorry—and then he and I could do the poster together. But there was no sign of him.

I chewed that fight over and over in my head like a dog with a bone as I sat on the step. I was sure I was right and who did Potso think he was, telling me what I could do and not do with *my* idea? But...he'd helped me so much, it was almost his plan as well. He'd come with me to the river to make the clay cow. He'd sat with me outside the shop when everyone laughed at us. He'd made the posters and encouraged me when I nearly gave up. He'd teased me, made fun of me. He'd even hit me with a rolled up poster—but he'd been next to me all the whole time. He and I had done everything together for so many years. Without him, this plan felt pointless.

And, to make it worse, he was right: the wheelbarrow really was a piece of junk. The bowl part was rusted right through and the wheel was not just flat. It was just a big flap of torn rubber that flopped in the dirt like the tongue of some dead animal. I didn't even have the tools to fix it. Could you fix a wheelbarrow with a fork and a bit of twisted wire? I didn't think so.

My grandmother spoke from where she was sitting under the peach tree. "Boi, you must learn to bear your own troubles."

"I am bearing them. I haven't spoken at all!"

"Hmm," she huffed. "I can hear your silence from where I am sitting."

You can't argue with a person who says things like this. It's like trying to pick a fight with Cedarville Mountain.

I watched her. She was hunched over her sewing, aiming the needle like it was a blunt stick through black fabric that she held right up to her face. It looked very difficult.

"What are you doing?" I asked her.

"Sewing the hem on my skirt for church."

"Can I help you?"

"No."

"I can help."

"No, you can't *help*. You can do it." She held out the needle and thread. "Come on. A boy needs to learn to sew just as much as a girl. There's nothing more irritating than a helpless man."

It was not fun sewing the hem. My stitches were big and untidy and the thread kept getting knots in it. I don't have a hand for sewing—or anything else for that matter. I was relieved that my grandmother would not be able to see the mess that I made. Black thread on black fabric is difficult to see even if your eyesight is good.

It was not fun drawing the poster for the wheelbarrow by myself either. I wasted about three sheets of paper from my exercise book until my grandmother asked me if I had a paper factory in the garden that she didn't know about. The end result was not impressive, but there was a caption to help: *Wheelbarrow to trade for anything of a higher value*— just in case someone thought I'd drawn a one-wheeled teapot or something.

Then I wasn't sure whether to add Potso's phone number to the poster, if he wasn't going to be involved any more. I imagined someone phoning the number to the broken phone and, instead of the message "The number you have dialed does not exist," it would say. "The friend you had does not exist,"—but I wrote it down anyway—because it was unthinkable not to. One day that phone *would* work. And Potso and I would be friends again.

But I went to sleep that night with a heavy heart.

SAY CHEESE

Potso ignored me at school the next day. I stood right behind him in assembly and could hear him and Mawili talking about the soccer game and Aviwe's progress, as if it was just their idea that Aviwe was now playing soccer for the Under 15s. It irritated me so much that I decided to just ignore him as well.

But I planned to go round to his house after I'd put up the new wheelbarrow poster outside the shop. Maybe I could apologize. People were starting to ask me every day what was happening with my trading game, and I wanted to keep the rhythm going. If someone made an offer for the wheelbarrow, I'd really have to make a quick plan to fix it.

When I got to the shop, there was no one there except Mam' uZungu. It looked as if she'd been waiting for me. She was carrying a ragged blanket which she begged me to take—although she said she had no need for the wheelbarrow. She thought the offer of free transport through to Kokstad was still available.

"Please," she begged. "I really need to get to Kokstad to go to the hospital. I need treatment and I don't have money for the taxi fare. Please! You can take my blanket."

"I am sorry, Ma. I've already made the trade and…" I raised my hands to show how empty they were. "Please, Ma, keep your blanket." I helped to arrange the ragged thing about her shoulders while she just stood there, full of despair.

I felt hopeless too when I saw how thin she was. She had a sore in the corner of her mouth and her eyes looked red and painful. She scared me.

Then Mkhul' uGaba came out of the shop, carrying a small bag of maize meal. He took Mam' uZungu by the arm and they walked together down the steps and along the pavement—slowly and painfully.

I stood by the wall where I hung up the poster and was so busy digging a hole in the dust with the toe of my school shoe and thinking about what had happened to the mobile clinic that used to come twice a week from Matatiele, that at first I didn't hear Jude calling me from across the road at the garage.

"Boi! Boi!" he yelled until I turned to look at where the noise was coming from. "There's a lady inside the shop!"

"Ja, so?" I shouted across the street.

"She wants to talk to you."

"Me? Why?"

Jude shrugged and turned away.

So I went in the shop to find out.

There were two strangers talking to Mrs. Viljoen: a lady with a notebook and a man with his long hair in a ponytail and a camera.

"There he is," said Mrs. Viljoen, pointing at me. "That's Boipelo."

The lady tucked her notebook under one arm and put out her hand to shake mine, which confused me. I'm not used to shaking hands with grown-ups.

"Boipelo, nice to meet you. I'm Lucinda Jacobs, a journalist from the *Kokstad Advertiser*," she said. "I have heard about your trading scheme and I wondered if you would mind if I write a story about you for our paper."

I didn't know what to say. I've never been interviewed for anything before. I rubbed the back of my leg with my foot.

"It's okay. You don't have to look so guilty!" She laughed. "Doesn't he look guilty? Eish! But you've done nothing wrong!" She thought it was very funny.

"How did you find out about me?" I was confused.

"Us journalists have our ears to the ground. We have our 'sources.'" She made two inverted commas in the air with her fingers. "Can we go somewhere quiet to talk, somewhere that we can..."

But the photographer with the ponytail interrupted her: "I just want a picture of Mrs. Viljoen here with the clay cow while the light is still good. Then can I have a picture of you, Boipelo, posing outside? Perhaps against the wall?"

Mrs. Viljoen took off her glasses and patted her gray curly hair. She picked up the clay cow and held it against her cheek as if it was a kitten and gave a funny little laugh. The photographer snapped away: *clickclickclickclick.*

The whole thing happened so fast and before I knew it, I was standing stiff as a pole outside against the wall beside the pathetic poster of the wheelbarrow I'd just put up.

"Smile!" said the photographer. "Say CHEESE!" And his camera went *clickclickclickclick* once more. But I could not smile.

If anything unusual happens in this village, you can expect that a crowd of children will be there to witness it within seconds. You won't know where they've come from or how they know to gather for the show, but they will be there as certainly as the sun will rise each morning. The crowd that gathered to watch me have my photo taken was a very lively one.

"CHEESE!" Some of them copied what the photographer said. "SEXY TIME!" said others and they posed with their hips jutting and their heads thrown back. Everyone was laughing and posing and jumping up and begging the photographer if they could also be in the newspaper. The whole thing got completely out of hand.

Eventually the photographer gave up trying to get me to "just relax and smile" and asked if I knew of a place where they could talk to me in private, so I led the way to the library, which is just behind the town hall. A long line of children followed us there.

Auntie Shirley would not let the other children into the library. She shooed them away so they all gathered to stare through the window, but the more she flapped her hands and tried to get rid of them, the more faces appeared.

Lucinda Jacobs and I sat at a table and I did my best to answer her questions, even though my mouth felt dry with nerves. I showed her the article from the old *You* magazine, which was looking very worn and ragged because of the amount of time it had spent in my pocket. And I took her through the trades from the clay cow to the Coke to the position of goalie to the free transport to the wheelbarrow.

"So you want to get a house, hey?"

"Yes."

"And you say that your friend helped you?"

"Yes. Potso. P-o-t-s-o Sebetso." I spelled out his name for her so that she got it right.

"And what does *Potso Sebetso* want to get out of this?" she asked. The way she said his name made it sound like she was laughing at me.

"I don't know. He just wanted to help me."

"Well, maybe he can visit you in your new house." She smiled at me as if I was a child who still believes in Father Christmas. "If it ever happens, hey?"

SHADOWS ARE GATHERING

After the interview, I went straight to Potso's house. Having to answer all those questions by myself made me realize how much I missed having him beside me. Without a friend, some things just feel pointless. It's like trying to play soccer by yourself. I wanted to talk to him. I wanted to say I was sorry and ask him to help me again. But Potso's mother said he wasn't at home. She thought he was at choir practice. So I ran on to Mrs. Jafta's house.

I peeped through the window. And Potso was there. He was standing right next to Sesi. Their shoulders were touching. And he looked as if he didn't have a care in the world.

Softly and tenderly, Jesus is calling, calling for me and for you...

I didn't want either of them to catch sight of me, so I ducked my head and sat with my back against the wall and just listened to the music as it came floating out of the window. I looked at my school shoes as they stuck out in front of me. They weren't going to last me long: the sole was peeling away on my right foot, the toes were scuffed, and the laces had snapped a long time back and been replaced with string. I had no socks.

Come home, come home
You who are weary, come ho-o-ome,
Earnestly, tenderly Jesus is calling,
Calling O sinner come home!

Home? There was nothing waiting for me at my home except a rusty old wheelbarrow that no one would want and a bad-tempered grandmother.

Shadows are gathering, deathbeds are coming,
Coming for you and for me.

There's a funny thing about death. You know it's coming, but you go around every day doing your business like you don't really know it. But sitting under that window, looking at my old shoes, I had the strangest feeling that it was really, *really* going to happen to me one day. It seemed incredible. I remembered Mkhul' uGaba in the shadows listening to the rehearsal on Saturday evening. Death was coming for him and for Mam' uZungu. How did they feel, knowing that this was close? I tried to imagine. Just thinking about it made me feel as if someone had stuffed me in a small, tight little box from which there was no escape.

The song ended and I imagined Potso and Sesi coming outside to find me sitting in the dirt under the window. So I got up quickly and kept low so I wouldn't be spotted. Home might be depressing, but it was better than being caught sitting under the window like a loser.

The streets, matching my mood, looked gray and desolate in the evening light. I hugged my arms in my threadbare school jersey. I realized that I'd stopped looking at houses—proper brick houses with chimneys, gardens and space—in the hope that one day I'd live in one. I still told people that I wanted to get a new house like Kyle MacDonald—but in my secret heart I could not imagine that it would work out. I'd be stuck in the trading game forever; going round and round, never upwards, always making the wrong trades and, because everyone knew about it now, too embarrassed to stop. Everyone else I knew lived in tiny, badly built houses with thin walls, broken windows, and small yards. Why should my life be any different?

Even Mr. Tshezi's house, with its dull solar-lit light-bulb, when looked at in the fading light, was depressing. His yard was always a terrible mess. There were old drums, hub caps, balls of tangled wire, rolls of moldy carpet, poles, electrical cables, old tires and all the rubbish that other people chuck out. He uses most of the stuff eventually, but it didn't look good.

I could hear the *tap-tap-tap* of a hammer somewhere in the direction of his roof—and then he stood up and I saw him silhouetted against the evening sky. The stars were just coming out and the moon was rising over the mountains beyond the Cedarville flats. There followed a rolling noise of something tumbling and I just caught sight of the hammer as it hit the ground.

"Nxa!" Mr. Tshezi clicked in frustration.

I opened his creaky gate and went to retrieve the hammer for him. But he was already climbing down the ladder. I stood waiting for him and handed it over.

"It's too dark up there. If I carry on, I will be falling off that roof next and then you'll have to take me through to the Matatiele hospital in many pieces." He wiped his hands on the greasy cloth that he tucked into his trouser pocket.

"Have you come about that cell phone?" he asked. "Your friend Potso was here earlier, but I told him he needs a new battery, and I'll have to order it from the supplier in Kokstad."

I shook my head. But just like that, when I thought I'd spent all my good ideas, I got another—and then another.

"That phone. What will it cost to fix?"

"About three hundred and fifty rand. Your friend said he can't afford it, so it's just sitting there." He jerked his thumb in the direction of his house behind him.

"Three hundred and fifty?" It sounded like a ridiculous amount of money but I hesitated only briefly before the words just popped out: "Can you order it? The battery? I will pay for it though it might take me some time to get the cash."

Was I crazy? I had no idea where I was going to get a fortune like that. Potso might have thought I was all talk and no trousers, but I was determined to prove him wrong. More than anything, I wanted to see his face when I handed him back a fixed phone. I wanted to be there and hear him laugh out loud when the phone actually rang one day.

Mr. Tshezi nodded. He was used to people taking a long time to pay him. "What's the other favor?"

"There's this old wheelbarrow. I need to borrow some tools, and I need someone to help me fix it up."

"Is this for your trading thing I've heard people talking about?"

I shrugged. "It's just a silly idea I had. It won't work. I'm just making a mess."

"Haibo!" Mr. Tshezi seemed irritated. "Mess is where everything starts. If I didn't make a mess, you think I'd ever get anything done?" He waved his arm over the chaos of his yard. "Anyway, you know what they say? Aim for that..." He pointed his finger at the moon that peeping out from behind ragged clouds "And if you miss, you might hit a star."

A star seemed a bit out of reach for me. All I needed was a wheelbarrow that worked.

Mr. Tshezi said he would help me as long as I didn't mess up his tools. We agreed that I would bring the wheelbarrow round after school the next day.

But I ran home with a little bit of the old feeling of excitement and possibility that—just ten minutes earlier—I thought I'd never feel again in my life.

CHICKEN

So after school I pushed that wheelbarrow with its flat tire along the road to Mr. Tshezi's house. The *flop-flop-flop* sound made by the old rubber made people laugh as I passed them. But I just kept my head down and pushed on to Mr. Tshezi's house.

He handed me a screwdriver and some rusty old metal cutters and said I could help myself to anything in his yard if I got his permission first. Then he attended to the flat wheel, which he did by taking a solid rubber wheel off an old pram and, with some spanners and some grease, fitted it to the wheelbarrow. He got it spinning perfectly.

I found a reflector strip, an old side mirror from a rusty car chassis, a number plate and a sheet of metal to fix the rusty bucket. I used the metal cutters to cut up cool drink cans to make flashes for the wheel. And I discovered that you can turn anything, even a pile of old junk, into a thing of beauty if you have some nails, wire, a hammer and someone who knows how to weld.

AmaZulu people make these cool trousers and matching waistcoats: khaki and covered in bright patches of red, green, and yellow with bits of braid. We call them umblaselo. My wheelbarrow was like an umblaselo wheelbarrow, all patched and decorated with its own reflector strips, number plate, hooter, a rear view mirror, wheel flashes —and the best thing about it was that it was sturdy and strong. It worked.

I was quite proud to wheel it to the shop after school the next day.

I noticed that the wall where I put up my posters was being used by other people too as a notice board.

- *Kittens to go to a good home.*
  Contact Pienkie at the Farmer's Co-op.
- *Lift wanted to Durban on Saturday.*
  Speak to Kolotso 443 Mzingisi.
- *Model needed to show off traditional*
  designs at the talent show.

There were the usual troublemakers outside the bottle store and a band of children looking for fun, fooling around and rolling down the bank. But Mrs. Viljoen didn't seem to mind them so much anymore. Maybe she was getting more customers from all the people coming to read the notices stuck to the wall.

Some of the little children hopped into the wheelbarrow as soon as I parked it and demanded a ride.

Mawili and Jude took turns pushing them up and down the pavement in front of the shop, while I sat under the poster trying to look like the guy in charge. Actually, I was scanning for Potso or Sesi.

I saw Sesi crossing the road opposite the town hall and heading towards the café. My heart almost stopped. Most other girls moved in little packs, their arms hooked together, giggling. But Sesi didn't always. Often I saw her doing something on her own.

She waved at me and pointed at the wheelbarrow as if to ask, "Is this yours?" I nodded and kept nodding until I remembered to stop. If Potso had been with me, he would have said out of the corner of his mouth, "OK, you can stop nodding now. You look like one of those silly nodding dogs that people put in the back shelf of their car."

But Potso wasn't there.

Luvo, who'd once offered me an old pie plate for my clay cow was talking to Sesi. That made me sit up and pay attention. He pointed at my wheelbarrow and leaned in to talk to Sesi too close for comfort. It's funny: Sesi is about thirteen and he's maybe twenty, yet something about her makes people ask her for advice.

He turned suddenly and took the stairs three at a time, coming to talk to me.

"Boi, bro!" he said, clicking his fingers.

"Oh, so I'm your bro now, am I? Just last week, I was an idiot with a clay cow that you thought was so funny, but OK…" Of course, I didn't say that out loud. I'm twelve and he's, as I said, about twenty, and that was how it was going to stay.

"I really need that wheelbarrow." He jerked his thumb behind him and we both watched Sesi take charge of the children. She was getting them to line up for turns in the umblaselo wheelbarrow.

"I need it because I have this idea. You know when people come back with all their heavy shopping from Matatiele or Kokstad?"

I nodded. I knew only too well the difficulties my grandmother has trying to get her bulk bag of mealie meal and five-liter bottle of cooking oil home, when the taxi rank is a couple of kilometers away from the house. Many times I'd had to be a pack donkey for her and carry the mealie meal while she balanced the five-liter container on her head. Lots of people buy in bulk from the wholesalers in Kokstad or Matatiele and then they are forced to leave their stuff at the taxi rank while they take the first load home. Sometimes they get back to find thieves have made off with their groceries.

"If I have that wheelbarrow, I can charge money to help transport."

I had to play this cool and not look too excited so I narrowed my eyes and dropped my voice a few octaves: "Ok, what can you trade for it? This is high quality. Not just any wheelbarrow."

Luvo came closer and pulled a small plastic packet from his jacket pocket. I peered at what looked like a bag of dead weeds.

"It's good stuff," said Luvo. "Pure Durban poison."

"Dagga!" I jumped back like it was a hot coal. All

attempt at being cool disappeared. "I can't trade in drugs! I'll get into trouble."

Luvo clicked his tongue impatiently: "Nxa!" He turned away. I watched him go back down the stairs to where Sesi was standing with one hand on the shoulder of the little girl who was next in line for a ride. Luvo talked to her and pointed back up at me and shook his head. Sesi shook her head. What were they saying? Probably that I was an idiot for refusing this trade.

But suddenly Luvo turned on his heels and jogged off down the road. Sesi looked up at me and put her hands together as if in prayer. Was she thanking me for not taking the bag of dagga? Was she asking me to be patient? Was she praying Luvo would come back with something better than dagga? I didn't know, but there seemed to be some kind of agreement between us, and I wasn't going to break it—whatever it was—for anything.

Not even for Mr. Retief who emerged from the shop with a newspaper and a liter of milk and stopped at the top of the stairs. "Who the hell does that thing belong to?" he asked while looking in the direction of my wheelbarrow. Everyone fell silent, even the children sitting in the wheelbarrow with their big eyes. We'd all trespassed in his old cheese factory and knew we were candidates to be locked in the cold storage room. Everyone was nervous to be around him.

"It's mine, Mr. Retief."

"Is this part of your trading scheme I've been hearing about?"

"Yes, Mr. Retief."

"I'll give you a 50 kg bag of mealie meal for that wheelbarrow. I could use it in my packing shed."

I knew that a bag of mealie meal bought at the Rhino Cash and Carry in Kokstad cost about three hundred and fifty rand. I glanced at Sesi and she shook her head just slightly.

"Mr. Retief, I've already made the trade." I looked down at the ground to show that I meant no disrespect.

He slapped his thigh with the newspaper, got into his bakkie and drove off, engine roaring, in the direction of the Farmer's Co-op.

This trading thing was much harder work than I ever imagined. I thought it would be easy, but it was like juggling snakes. There were the people I wanted to please, the people I wanted to avoid, the worry that someone was going to come with a better offer, the constant risk of making a fool of myself.... It was even harder making these decisions on my own. Where was Potso? He was always so good at these things.

And then Luvo was back—with a live chicken under his arm. And I was relieved that Potso *wasn't* there to see me trade a perfectly good wheelbarrow for a chicken worth about a hundred rand, when I could have made three times that with a bag of mealie meal. Kyle MacDonald did some risky trades but his trajectory was generally upwards. My trades were just going round and round, like water going down the plug hole.

But when I saw Sesi's radiant face, I knew I'd done the right thing. I took the chicken and Luvo raced down the steps to claim the wheelbarrow. He took it for a quick spin along the pavement, up and down in front of the shop.

A woman carrying two candles and a tin of fish came down the steps and to her surprise, Luvo stopped dead in front of her, bowed, took her tiny pile of groceries and placed them carefully in the wheelbarrow.

"No charge," he said grandly. "This is an advertising run. Tell your friends that I'll be at the taxi rank tomorrow to carry their shopping. But tomorrow I charge."

Then to the woman's even greater surprise, he scooped her up, put her just as carefully in the wheelbarrow with the groceries, and trotted off down the road with his first load—while everyone cheered.

ADDED VALUE

I walked home with the chicken tucked under my arm. It felt good to have another living creature beside me. I thought about not trading it and keeping it as a pet.

"I know you're not worth very much," I said to the chicken as we walked. "But thanks to you, I got Sesi to notice me. Did you see the way her face lit up when I gave Luvo the wheelbarrow? Maybe now she thinks I'm a good person."

I glanced down at it and I knew right away that a chicken wasn't a good substitute for a friend. A chicken won't tease you or wait outside a corridor while you talk to a teacher. It won't draw your posters or laugh at you when you don't want to laugh at yourself.

I imagined what Potso would say when he knew the deal that I had passed up for this scrawny hen. I hoped that he would be waiting for me when I got home and that we'd able to laugh about it together.

But he wasn't there.

"Has Potso been here?" I asked my grandmother.

"You know I haven't heard Piet and Potso for a few days. It's been very quiet around here. And no, I haven't seen Potso. But I don't see much. He might have been sitting right there on the doorstep, and I wouldn't have known."

I felt sorry for the chicken so I gave it some water in a tin bowl and a small pile of mealie meal. It just sat in the dust looking too shocked to eat or drink. My day had been stressful, but its day had probably been worse: first clenched under Luvo's sweaty armpit and then mine. It probably knew it was going to get eaten soon.

"Sorry, chicken," I said to it. I was going to tie its legs together but thought it had suffered enough for one day so I just tied the string around one leg and tied the other end to the trunk of peach tree so it could find some shade and reach the water and mealies if it needed to.

I went to get the ball point pen and tried to make another poster. I was on my fourth attempt when my father came home. He sat on the step and pulled off his work boots.

"There's a chicken under the tree," he said.

"No, there isn't," said my grandmother.

"Yes there is," he insisted.

"It's mine," I said, quickly, to put an end to this point-less conversation.

"You traded that wheelbarrow for a chicken?"

I nodded.

My father just laughed bitterly. "Yoh!"

I didn't want to hear any more about leaking buckets and broken dreams. Anyway I didn't need him to tell me it was a bad trade. I knew it.

But every now and then, my father surprises me.

"Maybe you need to think about adding value to this ...chicken." The way he said "chicken" made it sound like it hardly qualified for the title.

"What does adding value mean?"

"When I worked at the cheese factory, we had ways of adding value to the cheese so we could get more money for it. If you slice cheese, for example, you can charge more money than if you sell the same quantity of cheese as a block. Or you can sell the cheese already grated. Or cook something with it, like cheese sauce. That's called adding value."

"Ok, so if kill the chicken and pluck it, it will be worth more?"

"Yes, that's how it works."

"I could even cook it. Kyle MacDonald traded his Coleman stove with the offer of a cooked meal."

"If you knew how to cook." My father sighed as if he had the weight of the world on his shoulders, put both hands on his knees and heaved himself up off the step to fetch the basin to wash.

Behind him in the kitchen, my grandmother was chopping the green weeds we call imifino for supper. She used to collect it herself from where it grows wild beside the main road to Kokstad. But because of her bad eyesight, she now pays Sis' uNomazizi to pick it for her when she goes to harvest the weeds for her family.

Cooking can't be that hard, I remember thinking. *If even your blind grandmother can do it.*

I needed a new poster so before I went to bed I drew a pot with bits of chicken sticking out. It was easier than trying to draw a live chicken.

But that night, I had terrible dreams: I dreamed that I had moved into a big house, but it was dark and had a long passage. Potso was banging at the door and shouting at me to let him in. When I went to open it, I found the whole of Cedarville trying to give me things to trade and stuffing things through the windows: broken toys, library books, crocheted doilies, bags of dagga...and everyone was screaming at me. The photographer from the *Kokstad Advertiser* was shouting, "SAY CHEESE!" and my father was bellowing, "NO! DON'T SAY IT! SLICE IT! SLICE IT OR TURN IT INTO CHEESE SAUCE!"

I woke up feeling terrible. And it only got worse when I got to school.

POLITE CLAPPING

"Have you seen this, Boipelo?" Mrs. Jafta held out a newspaper as I walked into the classroom by myself on Friday morning. I'd just seen Potso, Jude, and Mawili giving Aviwe goalie practice in the playground and the way they all ignored me made me feel like I wanted to punch someone. Potso and I might have had our differences, but why were Jude and Mawili refusing to talk to me as well?

But when Mrs. Jafta showed me the story that had appeared in the Friday edition of the *Kokstad Advertiser*, the picture got a bit clearer...

There was a photo of Mrs. Viljoen holding the clay cow and smiling and another of me scowling in front of the Cedarville café. I looked like I'd been arrested and the photo had been taken by the police. The headline read: CEDARVILLE BOY TRADES CLAY COW FOR A BETTER FUTURE

I read the article softly under my breath.

Boipelo Seku, a 12-year-old boy from Cedarville, has decided to turn his life around, and in doing so he has single-handedly provided a lifeline of hope to a desperate village. Thanks to his unusual trading game, a disabled boy has been given the chance to play in a real soccer match and a teenage mother has been provided with free transport for a week to visit her sick daughter in hospital.

"My son was born with a club foot and although he loves soccer, we never thought he'd be able to play in a real soccer match," says the boy's father, local taxi driver Absolem Vezi. "Now his dream has come true."

According to Boipelo Seku, a Grade 8 pupil at the Cedarville Comprehensive School, "I got the idea from reading about a Canadian man Kyle MacDonald who traded a red paperclip on the internet. Each trade had to be of a higher value than the item he was trading. It took him 14 trades and eventually he was given a house."

Boipelo started trading with a clay cow which he made himself with river clay. He hopes to eventually be given a house in Cedarville...

I read on and just when I thought it could get no worse, it got worse...

According to this young man, the unexpected savior of Cedarville, people must take charge of their own destinies and stop complaining that no one is helping them. "Each person must take care of himself," said Boipelo Seku.

There was no mention of Potso, not one word. And why did she say that I had this idea about "taking charge of my own destiny?" *Destiny* wasn't a word I'd ever used in my life. And I had no problem with people complaining that their lives were hard. The article made me sound like I thought I was some kind of saint.

Mrs. Jafta must have read the misery on my face: "What's wrong, Boi? It's a wonderful story. You should be proud of yourself."

I just shook my head. "I never said that thing about people must stop complaining or that thing about destiny. And Potso isn't even in the story. Why didn't she say anything about Potso? I told her about him!"

"Journalists are famous for writing whatever they think people will want to read. You have to be careful what you say to them."

I left the classroom with the weight of the world on my shoulders and went back to the playground to look for Potso.

He ignored me when I called to him, so I had to go right up to the fence where they were playing.

"Potso!"

He still ignored me.

"Potso, I need to talk to you."

"You don't have to repeat yourself," he said over his shoulder as he ran past. "I was ignoring you the first time."

I pressed: "That story in the *Kokstad Advertiser*..."

Potso stopped running and stood hands on his hips breathing heavily: "...is all about how wonderful you are."

"That's what I want to talk to about. I never said anything about being the savior of Cedarville! And I told the journalist about you and how you helped me..."

"It's strange the way she didn't hear you."

Potso kicked the deflated soccer ball hard so it went sailing over the fence. He ran off to fetch it and left me feeling like I'd just been punched in the face. But with words.

Then the bell rang and we had to line up in the playground for assembly and we all had to listen while the headmaster gave us a talk about the talent show that was to be held that evening.

"You all know what is happening this evening at 7 o'clock. Mr. Sibaya from the Department of Arts and Culture in Mthatha is coming to judge the competition and the winners will receive sponsorship of an undisclosed amount. Hands up, those of you who have submitted entry forms. Please meet Mrs. Jafta after assembly for the program."

I looked down the line and saw Potso's hand go up, then Sesi's. I felt left out and wished that I'd thought of something I could contribute.

"Everyone is to wear their school uniform and behave themselves. No drinking, no fighting, no laughing—unless it's supposed to be funny—and no one is to throw things at the stage. When each act has finished, I want you to all clap like this..." He demonstrated by keeping one hand upright and with the other hand he tapped his palm lightly. He motioned to us to join in. Everyone did as they were told, and the patter of polite clapping washed over the playground—but the giggling told me that no one intended to do it like that at the concert. The headmaster was probably remembering the time when a ballet group came to the school earlier in the year and danced for us. Some of the boys lay down on the ground and tried to look up the ballet dancers' dresses and everyone roared with laughter because it was the first time we'd seen men wearing tights. Apparently, we were "disgraceful."

The talent show was the most interesting thing that had happened in our village for a long time—and just being in the audience was going to be as much fun as the acts themselves—but I didn't even feel like going. When you don't have a friend to sit with, where's the fun?

CHUCK NORRIS

Mrs. Jafta was locking up the classroom to go home when she stopped me.

"Sesi's been telling me that you traded with Luvo yesterday, your wheelbarrow for a chicken. Is that chicken still available?"

I said it was and told her what my father had suggested about adding value. "I'm thinking I'll offer to cook it for the person who wants to trade with me."

"That's an interesting idea." She picked up her bag of books and hoisted it onto her shoulder. "OK, Boi, I'll make you an offer. You have heard that Mr. Sibaya from the Department of Arts and Culture is coming to judge the talent contest tonight? Well, he's going to be staying at my house. How would it be if you cooked us that chicken for his dinner before the show? I'll provide all the other ingredients and you do the cooking. And in return...." She stopped walking and stared at the horizon. "In return, I'll give you a boxed set of Chuck Norris DVD's. How does that sound?"

"Eish! Does it have that one *The Delta Force?*"

"I know it has the first season of *Walker Texas Ranger.*"

A few years back, everyone told Chuck Norris jokes on the playground. *A very long time ago Chuck Norris gave the earth a good kick—and it's still spinning. Chuck Norris doesn't actually write books. The words just assemble themselves out of fear.*

There might be some truth in that last one, because just at the mention of Chuck Norris the words, "Yes, yes, of course, Mrs. Jafta. Thank you very much. What time shall I come to your house?" just assembled and came out of my mouth without any thought at all.

Maybe it was the Chuck Norris thing, but maybe it was the thought of spending a whole evening at Sesi's house before the talent show.

Mrs. Jafta looked at her watch. "It's 2 o'clock now. The talent show starts at 7, so let's say 4 o'clock. That should give you plenty of time."

I ran straight home and did something I'd never done before: I killed a chicken. I was glad my father wasn't there to see me screw up my face as I did it. He says if you eat meat, you have to be prepared to kill it yourself sometimes.

It wasn't easy. I tried to get my grandmother to do it for me, but she said it was about time I learned to do hard things for myself. She did tell me though that if I held the chicken upside down for a few minutes first, the blood rushes to its head and it doesn't panic so much and flap its wings. So I tried that—I covered its head gently with my hand and sang to it softly—and I was relieved when its body went soft and relaxed.

After I'd twisted its neck quickly, my grandmother took pity on me and offered to pluck it. She plunged it into boiling water and even though she could hardly see, her hands flew over that chicken carcass and within minutes she managed to remove even the tiniest pin feathers. Then with my face scrunched up, I cut off the feet and the floppy head and made a slit to pull out all the entrails. I reached inside the cavity and pulled out the warm liver, heart, and kidneys and left them in a small bowl for my grandmother to cook for our supper—and then I was done. It was over. I washed the bird under the tap and slung it in a packet, ready to go.

On the way to Mrs. Jafta's, I stopped at the café. There were the usual people hanging around and, although I didn't have a poster yet, I told them that Mrs. Jafta had offered to trade me the cooked chicken for the set of Chuck Norris DVD's. That caused excitement and a few of the children raced home to tell their parents.

On the way to Mrs. Jafta's house, a little girl ran up to me. "There's a man in a big silver Toyota with a Durban registration number who was looking for you," she said. "I told him to go to your house."

I didn't think much about it at the time. I was so busy

thinking about the real miracle that was about to happen: I would be spending a few hours in Sesi's kitchen. I didn't think about what I had to do in that kitchen. I was just pleased to have an excuse to be in it.

I passed the soccer field. Aviwe and his father were practicing for the big match tomorrow and I waved at them. They waved back at me and I was glad that someone still considered me a friend.

HACKING WITH A BLUNT KNIFE

"I've got pumpkin and cooking oil," said Mrs. Jafta, pointing to a pile of groceries on the kitchen counter. "And here is the salt, some onions, Aromat and carrots. And the rice."

"Rice?" Suddenly it sounded alarming.

Then she showed me where the knives were and banged a couple of pots on the counter top for me to use. Behind her, I could see Sesi in the garden, braiding her friend Joyce's hair. "And you'll need to use these pliers to turn the stove on because the knob has broken." I nodded, but had no idea what she was talking about.

"I'll just leave you to get on with it. I'm going to pick up Mr. Sibaya from the taxi rank. He's coming all the way from Mthatha so he'll probably be tired."

And she left.

I stared at the food and the pots on the counter,

but all I was thinking about was the fact that Sesi was standing just a few feet outside the kitchen door in a patch of late afternoon sun. I went outside to say hello.

"Hi!" called Sesi when she saw me. "Have you come to cook the chicken?" She stopped her work to stroke two cats that were curled around her ankles. "How are you going to cook it?"

"Oh, I'm to cook it with, er...rice. Rice and vegetables. You know, like a stew," I said casually as if I knew what I was doing.

Sesi and Joyce nodded.

"Well, I like boys who can cook," said Joyce. "I'm going to make sure I marry a good cook, because I am useless!"

It was about then that something snapped into focus, and I realized that I'd never made a chicken stew in my life. I'd seen my grandmother cook spicy "walkie talkies" and rice, and I wished I'd paid more attention. Should I cook the chicken first? Or the vegetables? Should I chop it or cook it whole?

"OK, I better get started." I backed into the kitchen hoping that if I just stared at the chicken, a plan would appear. But I kept looking out the window to watch Sesi as she put both cats gently in Joyce's lap and went back to her braiding. I had a vague idea that I should chop the vegetables first. So I chopped the carrots and onions and poured a lot of the Aromat and cooking oil over them. Then I hacked the chicken with the old knife. Next I attacked the pumpkin. Chopping a chicken and a pumpkin with a blunt knife is very, very hard work and I was sweating by the time I had finished. The kitchen looked extremely messy. There were peels and those papery onion skins everywhere.

I put the chicken in a pot, turned on the stove with the pliers as I'd been told, and turned my attention to the rice. Some of the rice slopped all over the floor on the way from the sink to the stove. I scooped it up with my hands and put it back in the pot.

The next half hour was terrible. The rice boiled over like a summer thundercloud pouring over Cedarville Mountain and spilled over the sides of the small pot. It kept burning at the bottom, so I added more and more water. And then the chicken: much of it was burnt before I thought of adding water and then I added too much. The burnt chunks bobbed about in the water like a horribly lumpy soup. In desperation I threw in the oily vegetables just as Mrs. Jafta came in the door with Mr. Sibaya from the Department of Arts and Culture.

"This is the boy I was telling you about, Mr. Sibaya—Boipelo Seku. He's cooking our supper tonight."

"Ah," said Mr. Sibaya, "I've been hearing wonderful things about you. It's very impressive when learners take initiative like you have done. Congratulations, young man." He held out his hand for me to shake.

I wiped my greasy chicken hands on my pants and shook his hand. This was the second person I'd shaken hands with in a few weeks.

When he'd gone to wash his hands for supper, Mrs. Jafta came back to the kitchen. She looked upset.

"What's going on in here, Boi?" She lifted the lids of the pots and looked anxiously inside.

"Mrs. Jafta, this cooking is more complicated than I thought."

"We can't eat this!" she said in an anxious whisper "I could never feed him this! We need to turn this stove off or we'll burn the house down." She flapped a dish-cloth. "Open the window to let the smoke out."

She carried the burnt pot of rice over to the rubbish bucket and dumped it so it landed with a dead thud.

"Now what am I going to feed Mr. Sibaya?" She opened the fridge and began lifting lids off bowls and sniffing the contents. "Ooof! I can't give him that, what-ever it was." She laid that dish to one side and lifted the lid on a new bowl. "Maybe this mince is still fine."

Mrs. Jafta turned and looked sternly at me, "Now Boi, what are we going to do with you? I can't give you those DVD's for this..." She waved her arm over the carnage. "I'm afraid the deal is off."

"I know. I'm so sorry, Mrs. Jafta." I did my best to tidy up: I swept the floor, soaked the burnt pots and got rid of the mountain of peels. But the damage was irretrievable.

Out of the window, I saw that Sesi was just adding the finishing touches to Joyce's braids.

I made sure I left the house through the front door before they came inside.

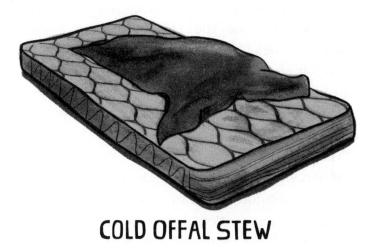

COLD OFFAL STEW

The whole thing was over. I had nothing to trade and it was my own fault. All I'd thought about was being in Sesi's kitchen and impressing her—and now she'd know what an idiot I was. As I walked up Station Road and past the houses, they seemed to shut me out, mocking me with their electric lights, tin roofs, their closed doors and their strong concrete walls.

"You'll never get one of us," they seemed to be saying. "This is what happens when you aim too high." The effort of trying to contain the tears that wanted to come made my throat ache.

Station Road was full of people streaming towards the town hall for the talent show: kids in their school uniforms, drum majorettes in tiny skirts and white boots, soccer players, parents in their Sunday clothes. I kept my head down to avoid seeing anyone I knew. I turned at the corner and walked past the town hall.

It was all lit up with the doors open wide. But instead of turning left to join the crowd, I just kept walking—against the tide of people who were arriving.

"Boi!" It was my father's voice calling from the other side of the road. "Hey! Are you coming or going?"

I crossed the road to talk to him and my grandmother who leaned heavily on her walking stick.

"I'm going. I don't feel like being at the talent show."

"Haibo, why are you behaving like a dog of the wind?" said my grandmother. I was, I knew, blowing all over the place with no settled plan, but it was too bad. The thought of sitting there clapping politely while other talented people like Sesi and Potso got to show off was not something I wanted to do that evening. Or ever.

"Nxa!" My Grandmother clicked her tongue to show her irritation.

"There was a man in a big silver car at the house earlier wanting to talk to you," said my father. "He said he was a journalist. I told him you'd be at the talent show if he wanted to talk to you."

Another journalist? I didn't want to talk to another one of those. I could still taste the shame of the last interview.

"I think he's wanting to talk to you about your trading scheme."

"Well, the trading thing is over. I'm not doing it anymore." I walked away without offering an explanation. I didn't need eyes in the back of my head to know that they were both staring at me.

My grandmother had left some of the offal chicken

COLD OFFAL STEW

stew in an enamel dish on the kitchen shelf. I ate it cold, like that was what I deserved, with a lump of pap, rinsed my dish, dragged out my mattress from under the bed, covered my head with an old blanket and went to sleep.

THE CLIMB

I woke when it was still dark, though I could hear the roosters starting up, so I knew dawn was coming. Softly, so as not to wake my grandmother who was snoring above me on the bed, I put on my big green jacket and my school shoes and let myself out of the door. I didn't want to face my father and get another lecture on the topic of leaking buckets, and I couldn't face Potso and was too ashamed to see Sesi. I had to get away, to a place where I knew I would not bump into anyone.

I jogged silently down the road, my breath making white puffs in the cold morning air. I slipped through the broken concrete fence that divides Khorong Koali Park from Mzingisi, took the road up past the big new Apostolic church and walked up Cedarville Mountain.

This mountain had always been part of the backdrop of my life. I knew the shape of it as well as I knew the

shape of my own foot or the back of Potso's head. I'd
hunted field mice on the low slopes, following a contour
path, but I'd never been beyond that. But climbing it
was harder, rougher and steeper than I'd imagined. The
slopes always looked smooth to me when I looked up
at it from the village, but when you are actually on the
mountain, the rocks, dongas and erosion make walking hard. It got easier as the sun rose and I could see—
though I made slow progress. I passed the white stones
that spell out CEDARVILLE 1888 and kept going.

Halfway up, panting and sweating, I sat on a rock
and faced the village below me. But I didn't really see
it. All I could hear was the noise in my own head: the
mocking and jeering jabber, the clatter of wounded
pride, stupidity, regret and vanity. Why had I told so
many people about my plan? Now everybody would
know what a failure I was! If changing a life was this
easy, other people would have done it. What made me
think I was so special? Why hadn't I asked for advice
about cooking that chicken? The thought of Mrs. Jafta
telling Sesi about how foolish I'd been made me groan
out loud. How would I ever patch things up with Potso?

I sat for a long time, holding my head in my hands
and staring at some dried grass in front of me. The
ground was parched and the grass had already been
bleached white by an early frost. Everything inside and
out was dry and lifeless.

But if you stare at a patch of ground long enough,
something is bound to come along eventually, even on
the slopes of the driest and most desolate mountain.

And there was an ant running around, waving its tiny antennae in the air. For the five minutes I watched it, it didn't stop its pointless scurrying: along a blade of grass, back on the ground, over stones, backwards, forwards, zig zagging round and round. When it hit a little obstacle, it stopped, waved its antennae, and hurried along as if it was late for a very important meeting. It didn't find a single edible grass seed or crumb of food. But still it ran around, waving its antennae. I bent down and let it run down my finger and across my hand. As soon as it reached the edge of my palm, I put my other hand alongside so that it scurried along that hand. I just kept transferring that ant from hand to hand so that no matter how fast it ran, it made no progress at all.

Suddenly...*waaak-waak-waak...*

The sound of Egyptian geese distracted me and I looked up to see three of them flying above me. They were so low, I could hear the lovely clean *whap-whap* sound of their wings. A sound like that rinses out your insides like a swill of clean water. I watched them head east to the river where the mist was hanging close to the water.

I could see the village of Cedarville spread out below me and it looked strangely orderly with its neat grid of roads, all signs of litter, mess, muddle and filth erased by the distance. I could see the shop where I'd put up my posters; our own small house; Potso's house with the tiny white van parked in the yard; Sesi's house and garden where I'd been just yesterday; the big square town hall with its red roof. I wondered briefly what had happened in the town hall last night? Who'd won the talent competition? What had Mr. Sibaya from the Department of Arts and Culture eaten for his supper?

I watched cars and bakkies driving along the main road, a taxi speeding in the direction of Matatiele, a trail of dust from a farmer's bakkie driving across the Cedarville flats. I tried to imagine where each one was going when my eye was caught by the flash of sunlight bouncing off the windscreen of a silver vehicle that looked shiny as a beetle. I watched it crawl slowly along the main road, turn off, and head for the Khorong Koali Park. A silver Toyota. Was this the same one my father and that little girl had told me about yesterday?

I watched as the vehicle swung slowly into my road and parked outside my house.

I don't even remember how I got down that mountain so quickly. Now it's just a blur of rocks, grass, boulders, dongas, tar, pavements, the pounding of feet and blood in my ears. But I do remember the relief I felt when I ran down our road and saw that silver car still parked outside my house. I flung open the gate and saw a large man with a big round face, sitting on an upturned plastic crate under the peach tree, talking to my grandmother.

"I'm Boipelo," I gasped for air. "My dad told me..." I doubled over, resting my hands on my knees to muster the breath to talk. "I want to talk to you. But you have to promise me something..."

FIRE MAKER

I was starting to notice something about myself when I spoke to people about this trading idea. If the person I was talking to thought that it was stupid, it felt stupid to me as well. I could read it in the person's face and something died inside me. All the excitement fizzled out like a fire made with wet willow wood, all smoke and no flame. It felt like that when I spoke to the journalist from the *Kokstad Advertiser*.

But when a person loved the idea, the opposite happened. The small fire crackled into life, and it wasn't just me who warmed myself at its little leaping flames, it was the other person as well. I've decided that some people put out fires and leave the world cold and hopeless, and others nurse the kindling, blow like mad, and fan the flames with whatever they have at hand—so that everyone feels its warmth.

This journalist from the *Sunday Times*, Musa Masela,

was a fire maker. He beamed at my story of Potso drawing the posters. He laughed. He clapped. He threw his arms in the air, and when I told him about the umblaselo wheelbarrow, he applauded as if I'd done something wonderful. And then I told him that I'd had to stop the trading scheme because I'd stupidly burned the chicken and had nothing left to trade—and his face expressed all the disappointment that I felt in my own heart.

"Hayi!" he shook his head. "Nah-ah. NAH-AH." He gripped his huge head in his hands, and I was afraid he would burst into tears.

"But I'm not giving up," I heard myself say because I could hardly stand his disappointment. "I'm going to earn some money, buy another chicken, and keep trading." I said it, but I had zero idea how I was going to do that.

Musa Masela got up off his chair with his fists raised above his head and did a little dance right there in the dust.

Even my grandmother laughed.

After we'd all drunk mugs of sweet tea, dunked chunks of bread and jam, taken photographs, and I'd checked and re-checked Potso's name had been correctly spelled, Musa Masela said that he had a job to do before heading back to Durban. He said he had a story to file.

"And where are you going *kwedini*?" he asked me. It felt nice to be spoken of as a young man.

"I have to earn some money. I have to buy a chicken."

And to myself I added, *And a phone battery.*

"Come on then, I'll give you a lift." Mr. Masela slapped my leg with his big hand.

I sat back in the deep leather seats in luxury while he cranked up the music. Sho Madjozi's rap song *Huku* came blaring out. Mr. Masela beat time on his steering wheel and had one elbow on the open window, so the whole village could hear. *Hukuniambia*, we both sang. I was grooving in my seat. Mr. Masela turned the music down a bit and told me that the lyrics were in Swahili. They were about a guy who was too scared to tell a girl that he loved her. As you can imagine, I felt powerfully sorry for the guy, whoever he was.

"I bet he didn't burn a chicken when he pretended that he knew how to cook," I said, looking out the window.

"So that's what happened, hey?" said Mr. Masela, looking at me sideways. "No, only a real idiot would do that!" He laughed and cranked up the music again. "We have to be brave." It was all very well for him to talk about courage, when he was driving a smart silver Toyota. With a big sound system. And one elbow resting on the open window.

He pulled up outside the shop, shook my hand, and slapped me on the back. I hoped that Potso or Sesi were somewhere around and would see me getting out of this smart car owned by this big important man, but they were nowhere to be seen.

"Kay sharp!" he said out of the window and waved as he did a U-turn, heading back in the direction of Kokstad.

SWEEPER

The village seemed strangely quiet for a Saturday morning. Then I remembered that it was the morning after the big night of the talent show. Who won, I wondered, and what was the prize? I'd forgotten to ask my grandmother. I'd been so distracted by talking to the journalist. I had my own dramas to worry about.

I trudged up the steps to the café, thinking I'd ask Mrs. Viljoen if she needed someone to sweep and pack her fridge with cold drinks. She already knew I was a hard worker.

But before I could enter the dark of the café, Jimmy Klaasens called my name:

"Boipelo! *Yiz' apha...*" He was sitting under the posters and had his hand resting on a rusty old bicycle that only had one wheel.

"Do you have those Chuck Norris DVD's to trade? See, I have this very nice bike that's..."

"No, Mr. Klaasens, I don't have the DVDs. I'm sorry."

"What? But this bike is worth a fortune. You'd be lucky to get this bike"

"I know, I can see that," I said, eyeing the cracked frame and the metal stump that was all that remained of the missing pedal. He'd probably got it off the dump. I doubted that even Mr. Tshezi would be able to rescue a bony old beast like that.

My eyes were drawn to the posters that had multiplied on the wall behind him. I scanned them quickly but most of them were people needing things: lifts, storage space and other boring things. But there was one: *Temporary job: sweeper needed in Mr. Retief's packing shed. R75 a day.* I couldn't believe my eyes! I ripped it off the wall in case someone else saw it and got to Mr. Retief's office before I could. As I turned to run down the steps, I remembered the talent show.

"Who won the talent show?" I asked Mr. Klaasens over my shoulder.

"Last night? You mean you weren't there?"

"No, I didn't go."

Mr. Klaasens laughed bitterly. "No one won. Everyone had to go home."

"Seriously?"

"Ser-i-ous."

He slung the old carcass of the bike over his shoulder. As he walked with me down Station Road, he told me the whole story.

The talent show had been late in getting started. I did wonder if that had been because of the delay in the supper. Mr. Sibaya had sat at a table right in the front of the stage with his back to the audience, but Mr. Klaasens said he was sitting in the front row and if he turned his head, he could see Mr. Sibaya's face clearly from where he was sitting. The first act were the drum majorettes. Mr. Klaasens swung his thin hips and twirled an imaginary baton. Apparently they were half way through when Mr. Sibaya started to look a bit strange and poured himself a big glass of water from a jug on his table. Then he drank another glass and Mr. Klaasens said he started wiping the sweat off his brow with the crocheted doily that was supposed to cover the water jug. The act ended. Everyone clapped, whistled, yelled and stomped their feet—whereupon Mr. Sibaya grabbed the empty water jug and vomited into it. Mr. Klaasens demonstrated by pretending to throw up into one of his hands.

"So that was the end of the talent show," he said with a big shrug and adjusted the bike on his shoulder.

"But why couldn't they get someone else to judge it?"

"Are you crazy? Every single person in that hall was known to the performers. Nobody would have trusted the result."

I knew what had happened. Mrs. Jafta had probably fed Mr. Sibaya the dodgy mince from that dish in the fridge. So the failure of the talent show had been my fault.

"So nobody won the sponsorship?"

Mr. Klaasens looked at me sideways and spat on

the grass: "You know what it was going to be? That so-called sponsorship? It was peak caps. With a logo on the front." He made a circle with his finger on his forehead. "That thing that says 'Department of Arts and Culture.'" He clicked dismissively. All that practicing and excitement for peaked caps! No wonder the village had a disappointed air about it.

"OK, when you have something to trade, you come and see if I've still got this bike. I might have sold it by then. It's worth quite a lot, so you will have to offer me something good."

Mr. Klaasens crossed the road and headed for Dark City—and I turned left near the railway line to seek my fortune with Mr. Retief.

LOCKED-IN

My heart was hammering when I stood outside Mr. Retief's office. I knocked very softly, almost wishing he wouldn't be there.

"Ja!" he shouted. When I opened the door, I saw that he was on the phone. He summoned me inside with his hand and swiveled his chair so that he had his big back to me. I sat down quickly. There was a lot of paper lying all over his desk, and there were piles on the floor. Everything smelled of fertilizer, creosote and dust.

"I don't care what your system is." He shouted at the person on the other end of the phone. "If you don't send me an invoice, I'm NOT paying!" He put the phone down hard.

"Ja?" he barked at me.

"Mr. Retief, I was wondering if you still needed someone for the sweeping job?" I unfolded the piece of paper that was screwed up in my hand.

"I thought you were too busy trading chickens and wheelbarrows and what-have-you."

I nodded and swallowed. "I don't have that chicken anymore."

Mr. Retief sighed. "Well, its not legal for me to be offering you work at your age. But I won't tell if you won't."

He took me through the shop to the packing shed that was stacked to the roof with sacks. He pointed at a wide, heavy, wooden broom and showed me where the rats had nibbled the corners of the bags so that dried mealies lay in drifts all over the huge concrete floor. He showed me the big tin dustpan and pointed at a black bin. "Just chuck them in there."

He looked at his watch. "It's late now and we close early on a Saturday, so I'm not going to pay you the full amount for today. You can come back on Monday after school and make up the hours." He strode out of the packing shed.

I picked up the big brown broom and started sweeping...and sweeping...and sweeping. Some of Mr. Retief's workers came in with a trolley, loaded sacks, and left me alone with my work. Rats had made a lot of mess and that storeroom was huge. It wasn't long before I got a blister at the base of my thumb. I stopped to examine it and when I looked up, there was a big rat sitting in the center of the floor. I gave it a mock charge with the broom raised above my head, but it just sat on its haunches and wiffled its nose. So I wiffled my nose back at it, no point in trying to scare it away. The more rats there were, the more mess—the more work and the more money I stood to make.

I sat down on a pile of sacks to rest and caught the sound of vuvuzelas coming from the soccer field behind the gum trees. The soccer match! Aviwe's game! I'd forgotten. I wanted to be there, but the thought of seeing Sesi and Potso twisted my guts. I got to my feet and swept as if I could brush away all the messes I'd made and dump them in a bin.

After some time, I realized that while it sounded very noisy outside—I could hear vuvuzelas, cheers, and even the referee's whistle, there was no sound coming from Mr. Retief's co-op. No workers had come into the shed for some time. The big door to the packing shed was closed and when I tried to pull it open, it wouldn't budge.

I'd been locked in!

Everyone had gone home and forgotten about me. I gave the door some half-hearted thumps with the tin dustpan, though I knew no one was out there to hear.

What was I going to do? I couldn't spend a weekend in a packing shed nibbling dried mealies like a rat. What would I drink?

There was a small window high up under the roof that could be accessed by climbing a tower of sacks, but would it open? I heaved myself up and saw that it was done up with wire and covered in big furry cobwebs. It took me a long time to work that wire loose with my bare hands and when I creaked the small window open and peeped out I could see the small herd of sheep that

Mr. Retief kept to crop the grass around the old cheese factory. They were below me. And through the gum trees, I could see the soccer field with a bigger-than-normal crowd. I could even see the donkeys tied to the fence.

But the ground was a long way down. Potso had told me once that if you can get your head through a space, you can get the rest of your body through. My head just fitted. But you don't want to go head-first out of a high window. So I turned myself around and wriggled my legs through first. After a lot of huffing, puffing and squeezing, my whole body was out, and I was hanging onto the window frame with my fingers. The only way down was...down.

So I let go—and hit the ground hard—and the sheep scattered.

I was dazed. But after a few moments, I stood up and waggled each leg and arm. It was a miracle that nothing was broken.

I looked for holes in the fence but Mr. Retief had wired them closed. So I found a likely spot and did some more unpicking until I'd made a hole big enough for me to wriggle through on my tummy.

I stood looking at the soccer match that I could see through the gum trees—and couldn't decide if I'd risk going.

Then two sheep trotted past me and bleated: *me-e-h-me-e-h*. I whipped round and saw the last of the sheep wiggling through the hole I'd made in the fence. The stones and clods of earth that I threw at their big woolly bottoms just made them trot faster in the direction of the station, so I waved them off. Mr. Retief would never know that I'd made the hole through which they escaped.

Something about those annoying sheep doing whatever they pleased, and perhaps the fact that I'd just survived jumping from a high window, made me brave. If I could survive that jump, I could survive going to the soccer match and facing the two people I dreaded. I knew I'd have to see them eventually. I didn't know what I would say to either of them, but the excitement of the game carried through the gum trees and over the road and was impossible to resist.

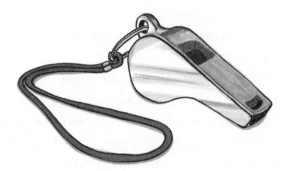

THE AFRICAN CUP OF NATIONS

It's always easy to see how a game is going and how close the score is just by watching the crowd and the coaches. The spectators at this game—Cedarville vs. Kokstad Under 15—were all on their feet and pressing so close to the game that some of them were actually on the field. Everyone was focused on the action in the Cedarville box. Coach Nontso was pacing anxiously with his hands behind his back and the Kokstad coach was yelling at his players to "Get forward!" I saw the ref looking at his watch. The Cedarville spectators were tapping their wrists and whistling loudly to signal to the ref to call the game. I'd arrived in the final moments.

"What's the score?" I squeezed in beside Jude.

"It's a draw. Two goals each. But this corner could change things."

A Kokstad player whipped in the corner kick and the players surged forward. There was a lot of scuffling and tussling and the dust made it difficult to see. The ball fell to a Kokstad forward who kicked it into the arm of an unsuspecting Cedarville player. Of course the Cedarville team cleared the ball and tried to look as if nothing had happened, but the aggrieved Kokstad players engulfed the referee with cries of "Penalty! Ref! Penalty!"

"Penalty!" shouted the Kokstad coach, his hands wide as if to say, "Come *on!*"

There was a hush as we waited for the ref's decision.

He blew the whistle and pointed to the spot.

"Aaaagh!" Jude held his head in his hands as if it was the end of the world, while all around us spectators moaned and shook their heads with the injustice of it.

"*Hayi! Suka!*" Some spectators flapped their hands to indicate that Kokstad should just go home and stop wasting our time.

Jude had his back to the field with both arms over his head and his eyes tightly shut as if he was braced for a crash landing. He could not bear to watch.

Aviwe's dad stood right behind the goal, giving him advice and pointing at his eyes with both index fingers. Aviwe nodded, waved his arms, and clapped his hands, poised for action. Potso had been right about the hundred percent. The Kokstad number 10 stepped up and placed the ball. From where I was standing, Aviwe's leg looked like a twig that might snap. There was no way he could save this penalty.

And this goal would be decisive.

The number 10 walked backwards to the edge of the box. Aviwe watched his every move through slit eyes.

A hush fell over the crowd.

The ref blew his whistle. *Briittt!*

The Kokstad player aimed hard for the bottom left of the goal—Aviwe dived—and incredibly, impossibly, wonderfully, he deflected the ball wide.

"Brriit brritt briiiiiiittttt!" The final whistle blew and the crowd went berserk: dancing, punching the air, hugging one another, surging onto the field and blowing on their vuvuzelas. Aviwe's father threw his sunhat on the ground and rushed round the goal to sweep Aviwe into his arms.

It was just a draw, but the way everyone carried on, you'd have thought Cedarville Under 15 had just won the African Cup of Nations.

Aviwe's victory made me even braver. I scanned for Potso in the crowd. It was a good time to make peace: no one could nurse a grudge in that carnival atmosphere. Everyone was milling about on the field, laughing and hugging one another and slapping Aviwe on the back. Chipo was even riding one of the donkeys, tapping it lightly with his heels so that it trotted up and down the field.

"Boipelo! *Yiz'apha.*" Aviwe's father called me over to where he stood with his arm around Aviwe in the goal.

"Well done!" I gave Aviwe a high five. "Great save."

"Where's that friend of yours, Potso?" There was no sign of him or Sesi. Sesi wasn't always at the soccer games but it wasn't like Potso to miss this one.

"Well, I want to thank you from the bottom of my

heart for giving my son Aviwe this chance." Aviwe's father pumped my hand and slapped my back so hard it hurt. "Because of your trading thing, this has happened." His arms swept over the scene of jubilation on the field. "Now we need a photo." He took out his cell phone.

But I was learning. The last thing I needed was another photo of me looking like I was taking all the credit for something I hadn't done alone. Aviwe's participation in the game had been more Potso's idea than mine.

"Let me find Potso. He must be in this photo too." I ducked his outstretched arm and ran off before he could talk me out of it.

"Where's Potso? Have you seen Potso?" I asked everyone, but no one had seen him.

I was just about to run to his house, when Mawili called after me: "Boi! I remember now. He'll be at Mam' uZungu's funeral. The choir is singing."

Mam' uZungu *died*? The shock stopped me dead. Why hadn't anyone told me? Oh man, I was sorry that I'd been so busy with the small dramas of my life. How had I missed this news? Sometimes you think if you just pay attention, you can stop bad things from happening. It's not true, but that doesn't stop you thinking it's possible.

FUNERAL

Saturday afternoon is always funeral time in this village. My grandmother had told me that in the old days funerals used to be a big deal: the family of the deceased would hire a tent and make huge pots of food. There would be lots of singing, fluffy blankets for the family members, wreaths of plastic flowers, and always a large framed photo of the person who had died. But then so many people died of AIDS. There were just so many deaths and people became poorer and poorer—and nowadays not many families can afford these big funerals. Some can't even afford two hundred and five rands for the coffin and someone has to go house to house asking for donations. I knew that someone had probably had to do that for Mam' uZungu. There would be no big pots of food, no fluffy blankets or framed picture for this funeral.

The graveyard on the edge of town faces the

Cedarville flats. There are no trees. Just dust and veld. It is a very lonely place. The municipality put up a tall metal fence with spikes because people were breaking graves and stealing the big marble headstones. But when bits of the fence got stolen too, they gave up— and now anyone can walk through.

I could see a small huddle of people on the far edge. As I got closer, I could hear snatches of the hymn carried on the thin sneaky wind.

Amazing grace...the sound...a wretch like me....

Dust swirled around the mourners made up of the choir, Mkhul' uGaba who was sitting in a plastic chair, Mrs. Jafta and a woman I'd never seen before. Perhaps it was Mam' uZungu's daughter who had come through from Kokstad. I wondered who had dug the grave. Usually it is the men of the family, but there were few who looked strong enough for that task. The priest, head bowed, shoulders stooped, was wearing a black dress over his ragged pants and dirty shoes. He held his Bible against his chest like a shield.

I stood on the edge of the group, a bit apart, and asked God to bless Mam' uZungu's spirit, wherever she was. And I asked Mam' uZungu to watch over us all. When I opened my eyes, I saw Potso looking at me but he looked away as soon as our eyes met—as quickly as two flints striking against each other. I realized that I couldn't try and talk to him in this place. If he'd been at the soccer field where everyone was hugging one another and laughing, I could have done it. But when you are standing at a grave, it doesn't feel right. There's something about funerals. I didn't want Potso thinking I was taking advantage. He might feel he has to forgive me, because when you are in the presence of death, everything else feels a bit stupid.

Also, I was so afraid. What would I say? We'd never had a fight before, and I didn't have the words. I didn't even know who was really to blame. I knew it wasn't my fault the journalist had said those stupid things in the *Kokstad Advertiser.* But I had made the trade with Sis' uDana without consulting him. I felt bad about that and decided that if we became friends again, I would not leave him out. We'd make all decisions together.

But somehow I knew that this fight was about something bigger, more complicated than that. And I had no idea what it was or how to fix it.

THE DOOR

It felt strange to go home alone and have no plans. At that time in my life, I didn't spend time at home alone with my father and my grandmother. It was just the place I ate, slept, washed and kept my clothes. I always had Potso with me and we did things—out of the house—together. Now home felt empty like an old pumpkin with just three seeds rattling in it.

As I came through the gate, my father grunted at me, which was his usual greeting. He was digging over rock hard soil against the boundary. So that he could plant the usual turnips and cabbages; he seemed preoccupied with the work. We didn't speak.

I wondered where my grandmother was—and then I remembered, it was month-end and she would be at the church for her savings group meeting. Nothing interfered with her attendance at her stokvel gatherings. On the last Saturday of every month, without fail, she put on her best black skirt, tied up her head in her brightest scarf, tucked a small amount of money into her blouse and set out with her walking stick. Once some of the amaphara, gangstars, tried to steal her money before she got to the church. She swung her walking stick and cracked one of them on the head. It never happened again.

I did ask her once what she was saving for—but I never got a straight answer. First she told me that the Bible tells us to cast our bread upon the waters—though why wet bread would ever be a good idea was not clear to me. Another time she told me she was going to spend it all on a trip to Durban to see the ocean before she died. But then I overheard her talking to Sis' uNomazizi about a trade school in Kokstad that took people who had a matric and offered apprenticeships to plumbers, bricklayers and mechanics. When Sis' uNomazizi asked about the costs, my grandmother said that she hoped when the time came she would have enough money for the registration fee and all tuition costs. So, I had a suspicion that she was saving the money for me to use one day. After all it wasn't very likely she was ever going to learn plumbing or bricklaying—and my father doesn't have a matric.

I fished out the old pile of *You* magazines from under the bed and sat on the step outside to read them. I'd never read anything just for fun before, but *You* magazine had got me into this mess, maybe it could get me out.

It didn't work: the longer I sat reading about Ronaldo

and his new house and the woman from Nelspruit who gave birth to co-joined twins, the lonelier I felt. I had this weird feeling that it didn't matter to my father if I was there or not. Would he even be interested in my escape from the packing shed? Should I tell him that I'd got my first job that morning? Did he know that Mam' uZungu had died?

It was late in the afternoon when I decided to walk to the river. Just for something to do. I couldn't sit looking at the pictures of Ronaldo's house with its marble staircase forever.

As I passed Mkhul' uGaba's house, he was seated, as he always was, on the broken plastic chair outside his door. He saw me and called my name.

"Boi! *Yiz'apha.*" He pointed at an old plastic crate by his fence and I fetched it, flipped it over and sat down beside him. He coughed for a while, then when he'd recovered his breath, he said: "I saw you at Mam' uZungu's funeral."

I nodded. "I'm sorry she's gone."

Grandfather Gaba closed his eyes and just sat rocking backwards and forwards slightly in his chair. "Ewe," he said.

We sat in silence for a long moment.

"And I saw you leave by yourself." He coughed more with his hand on his chest. The coughing seemed to exhaust him.

"I always see you with Potso. Boipelo and Potso. You go together. Like pap and milk. Or kota and chips." He held up his index finger on both hands and brought them together to touch.

He was right: I'd have said that Potso was the kota, the quarter loaf of white bread, and I was the chips that went inside the kota.

"We had a disagreement," I said.

He nodded.

"You are a young boy still, just an inkwenkwe, but one day you will see..." He coughed some more. I waited for him to finish.

An *inkwenkwe* is a young boy who has not yet been circumcised. You are only mature when you are about eighteen and you go off into the bush to live by yourself and go through the circumcision ritual. Then you come home and you are an *indoda*: a man. That time seemed a long way off for me.

"When you are an *indoda*, you must do things by yourself. Perhaps you will go somewhere to study or try to find a job. One day you might get married. You will do these things by yourself. If you try to take your friends with you everywhere in your life, you won't be able to move."

I'd never imagined a world without friends beside me.

"How old are you?" he asked me.

"I'll be thirteen soon."

"It is the time..." He put his hand on his chest to hold back the cough that wanted to come. "It is the time when friends might start pulling away."

He put his two hands together equally with both palms facing downward. He moved one hand so it pulled ahead and left the other hand behind.

"Sometimes this happens because one friend gets a girlfriend. Or because one discovers he is talented in some way and the other one isn't."

Potso was the one with talents—not me. I was never jealous of his talents. And I had none for him to be jealous of. So it didn't make sense.

"Sometimes one friend gets good fortune and leaves the other friend behind."

I'd always thought of Potso as so sure of himself, strong and confident. He was usually the one with ideas. Was my trading idea something that had made me go ahead of him? Had I left him behind?

"It is very hard when that happens. It hurts. In here." Mkhul' uGaba pointed at his heart. "But every person has something they must do. It's like a door that has your shape. Every boy and every girl has a door like this. Every person. But if you try to take your friends with you all the time, you will never fit through that door. Sometimes you must go alone."

He sat back against the wall, exhausted by his words.

"Only a few people find their door and go through it. Many people see their door but are too afraid to go through it alone. Some..." He coughed some more. "Some never find it because of personal circumstances. Then they drink or smoke or complain—they find fault with others—so they don't have to feel the pain of not finding it. You know those people: those who are dead while living."

I knew he spoke the truth.

"When a door opens for you, you must be willing to pass through it alone. People think it's important to have friends—and it is. But it's even more important to find the doors that have your shape and keep walking."

I waited while he caught his breath.

"It's hard in the beginning to walk alone, but people will respect you in time if you do this. And you will not always be lonely. The people who understand this will be your friends."

We sat quietly for a very long time. His explanation was the only thing that made sense to me. Perhaps I had a door to walk through and Potso had another. Would we meet up on the other side? I hoped so.

As I sat thinking, a crack opened in my mind and a new thought entered: maybe it was difficult for Potso to see me get all this attention and get my picture in the newspaper. Perhaps he worried that I *would* get a house and my life would be different to his. I knew I would have been worried if it had been the other way around. It's easy to be friends with someone when you are both struggling. I could see that it was harder when things go well for one person and not the other. I also knew that things were not going that well for me right at that moment—but Potso didn't know that I'd lost the chicken and made such a fool of myself.

Did I even know someone who had found their door and gone through it? It was hard to think of adults in this way. But Sesi...Sesi was someone who I thought would appreciate someone willing to go through a door alone. She always kept herself slightly apart from people. She had lots of people wanting to be friends with her, but there was something about her. She didn't try too hard, she did things when she wanted to, she didn't always move in a big pack like other girls.

I wanted to be a boy who would be brave enough to walk through his door alone.

Mkhul' uGaba seemed to be asleep. There was a cold wind so I went inside his house to find a ragged blanket to cover him. His chest was rising and falling, but I could see that every breath hurt.

He just nodded to thank me.

BOI WHO WALKS ALONE

On Sunday morning, I woke up, knowing that I had to keep going, to buy another chicken and keep trading, even though I didn't know where this zig zag path would take me. I also knew that I did not have to get Potso's permission for every trade, though I had decided that I would find him after church and tell him about all the things that had happened to me since we'd been apart. That thought scared me.

I knew that I hadn't been wrong to do that trade for the wheelbarrow without him, so there wasn't much point in apologizing. It's funny how when things go wrong, I always thought someone was to blame—but now I could see that, although things had gone wrong, it was hard to see who was at fault. It was as if our two stories had just crashed into each other—and the strange thing was, they were both true. My story was true for me and Potso's was probably true for him.

I wished I'd earned enough money to hand him back his fixed phone as a peace offering right away. But the money would take me a long time to accumulate and if I was going to be "Boi, who walks alone," I decided I had better get used to it.

I was sitting on the step outside our house, eating a bowl of pap and milk when Siyabulela, one of the small boys who lives at the end of our street, came running down the road, his small legs and arms pumping like pistons.

"It's Mr. Retief!" he shouted as soon as he saw me. "He's coming! He's coming to your house!"

I stopped eating and put down my bowl and spoon. I felt sick. I knew what had happened: Mr. Retief had discovered the hole in his fence and his missing sheep and was coming to...do what? Beat me? Fire me from my job?

His bakkie roared up to our house. Mr. Retief got out and slammed the door. He had a rolled up newspaper under his arm. Maybe he was going to whack me with the newspaper.

"Is your father here, Boipelo?" he asked gruffly.

"He's inside," I squeaked and scrambled off the step to call him. But my father was already at the door wiping his hands on a towel.

"Mr. Seku, we need to talk," said Mr. Retief.

My father beckoned him into our house. He shut the door and left me outside on the doorstep.

It was the longest five minutes of my life. I could hear the rumble of their voices talking inside but I could not hear what they were saying. All the feelings I'd woken up with, the determination to be "Boi, who walks alone", had abandoned me, and I was back to feeling like a small child in trouble.

Suddenly the door flew open and my father told me to come inside. I looked anxiously at his face to see if he was angry with me but could not interpret his expression.

Mr. Retief was sitting on my grandmother's bed. She was standing beside the kitchen sink in her church clothes.

There were a few moments of silence while they all looked at me. My heart was bouncing about in my chest like a tennis ball in an old oil tin. I sat on the floor by the door.

My father cleared his throat and said, "Boi, Mr. Retief has come to make a trade with you."

I was mystified.

"Mr. Retief, I have nothing to trade. Yesterday I told you that I've lost the chicken and..."

"You do have something to trade," said Mr. Retief. "Something quite valuable actually." The newspaper was open on the bed beside him. "Look here at this morning's *Sunday Times*." He tapped a page twice with his big hairy finger.

I got up and went over to the bed to see.

It was a big page spread and the headline read:
CLAY COW BOYS CHANGE LIVES

There were three photos: a close-up of me scowling that had been taken by the *Kokstad Advertiser*, a picture of Mrs. Viljoen standing next to her till with the clay cow stuck on top, and a picture of Potso grinning in his school uniform, a picture I had never seen before.

"Read the story," said Mr. Retief.

The story written by Musa Masela was about two boys from Cedarville, Boipelo Seku and Potso Sebetso, and how they had worked together on a remarkable idea to try and change their lives. Biopelo had the original idea and Potso drew the posters. They had done everything together and brought happiness to a few people in Cedarville: a disabled boy got a chance to play in a real soccer match; a teenage mother got free transport to visit her sick child in hospital; an unemployed man got a wheelbarrow to start a small business....The story even described how Boipelo had burnt a chicken and was determined to buy another one and start trading again.

I couldn't believe that I'd only met Mr. Masela yesterday and the story was already in the newspaper. It was a good story and one I could be proud of.

"I still don't understand, Mr. Retief. What can I give you? Do you want the chicken when I buy another one?"

"I don't want your chicken!" Mr. Retief looked indignant. "I don't think you realize what this kind of publicity is worth. This is the *Sunday Times!* It's not the *Kokstad Advertiser.* This morning, people all over the country from Boksburg to blimming Bloemfontein are going to be reading about you Clay Cow Boys today. People love reading stories like this when there is so much depressing stuff everywhere."

I was surprised. I'd never seen a *Sunday Times* before and Musa Masela had been so nice to me. How was I to know that he worked for such an important newspaper?

"When I read this story this morning," Mr. Retief continued, "I got an idea. I've been thinking about re-opening the old cheese factory and start making cheese again. But it seemed risky to start a business in a small village that no one has ever heard of. The costs of advertising would be too much. But now that Cedarville is getting quite famous, thanks to your strange trading business, maybe we stand a chance. But we have to move fast because people have short memories for these things. And the cheese will sell even better if you let me use your name."

"You want to call it Boipelo Cheese?" The name didn't sound that good to me.

"No, man!" Mr. Retief was irritated. "I want to call it *Clay Cow Cheese!* That's what I want to trade with you."

"But what will you give me in return?" I asked, still confused by his offer.

"Well, I can't give *you* much, I'm afraid," said Mr. Retief. "But I can offer your father a job helping me to set it all up. I could definitely do with his experience in cheese production. In fact, I can't do it without him."

I looked up. I was too pleased to speak. I nodded.

My grandmother put her hands together: *"Enkosi! Thank you, Jesus! Enkosi."* And she clapped her hands. I'd never seen her looking so happy.

"Don't just thank Jesus," said Mr. Retief. "Thank this child of yours."

We all laughed.

And just like that, I got another idea. Then another. Then another...

"Mr. Retief," I said, terrified, but willing to take a chance, because I knew I would not get another. "I have a favor to ask you."

"Hmmmm?" Mr. Retief looked at me and frowned so that there were deep grooves down on either side of his mouth. I thought I'd start with the easy one first, though my heart was still pumping. I had never spoken like this before in my life. I took a deep breath.

"Will you let me carry on working for you, sweeping in your packing shed? I still need to earn some money."

"Okaaaay." Mr. Retief nodded slowly.

"Also..." I said and swallowed. I was so nervous. Mr. Retief frowned even more. I could see he was worried if he agreed to another favor, it might never end.

"And...next time you go through to Matatiele, there's someone...Mkhul' uGaba. He is an old man who lives at the end of our road. Please can you take him to the TB hospital when you go to Matatiele."

Mr. Retief went through to Matatiele all the time to buy stock for his co-op. I didn't know why it had taken me so long to think of this.

"Ja, I will do that," he said and slapped his legs to get up off the bed to leave. As far as he was concerned, he'd given enough favors.

"And one more thing..." I'd left the biggest for last. Mr. Retief sat back down on the bed slowly and puffed air through his mouth as if to say, "Will this ever end?"

"If you need a van for the cheese factory, for deliveries and to fetch things...I know someone who has one—but it just needs a set of wheels."

"Hmm," he grunted. "I'll have to think about that one. Not making any promises."

When Mr. Retief eventually left, my grandmother looked at her huge watch by putting it right up against her face and realized that we were too late for church. She sat on the bed, her hands clasped, rocking backwards and forwards, still praising God for the gift of this job: *"Hawu, Nkosi-yam...Siyabulela!"*

I went to the door.

"Are you going out?" asked my father as he stirred his tea.

"I'm going to wait outside the church for when Potso comes out."

"Go," said my father and he looked me in the eye and put one hand on my shoulder. *"Mntwan'am."*

"Mntwan'am," I whispered to myself as I turned onto the Main Street. My father had never called me "my child" before. *Mntwan'am.* The feeling of it spread like warm oil all over my head, down my shoulders and along my arms as I walked.

FOUR MONTHS LATER

I stood in the shade of the big gum trees near the soccer field, feeling the warm late spring breeze. I was waiting for Potso to arrive for the grand opening of the Clay Cow Cheese Factory. From the outside, the factory didn't look that different, although all the broken windows had been replaced and the green roof had been repainted. But it was inside, where most of the work had been done.

My father, wearing white gum boots and white overalls, had taken me round the day before. I hardly recognized the place now that the floors had been painted white, doors re-hung, lights fixed and huge complicated stainless steel machines—vats, presses and pumps—installed. When he swung open the big heavy door on the brightly lit cold storage room, I was very quiet, looking at the gleaming shelves where once there'd been darkness, gray walls and the dread of being shut inside for the weekend.

From where I stood under the gum trees, I could see the new sign that had gone up just in time for the opening. It was wrapped in a big white sheet that would be pulled away for the big unveiling. I could also see the makeshift stage that stood in the sunlight. It was made from wooden pallets, guarded on both sides by huge speakers and embraced by rows of green plastic chairs. Some farmer's wives were unrolling long extension cables and setting up urns to boil water for tea in the shade of the building. Others, wearing aprons and fierce expressions, were guarding the large trays of food that lay under shiny tinfoil on the trestle tables.

Suddenly above me, I heard the *Piet-my-vrou* calling. Maybe because of the way my grandmother teased me when I made a noise, and call me Piet, I always felt a connection with this bird. I looked up but as usual I couldn't see it. I knew it would be hiding in the top branches. Despite its shyness though, the call, when it comes, is proud and clear. It travels far. This was the first call I'd heard that season, and I knew it meant that summer was coming.

Piet-my-vrou! Piet-my-vrou! I whistled, trying to copy it—but the bird went quiet.

Suddenly, I heard the sound of a car engine. A small white van raced down the dirt road towards me. It pulled up outside the cheese factory and Potso hopped out of the passenger seat. Mam' uSebetso climbed out on the driver's side. She was wearing white gum boots and white overalls, the same as my father's. On the side of the vehicle was a logo of a clay cow and the words *Clay Cow Cheese Factory.*

Potso opened the back door of the small van and no fewer than twelve soccer players, including Aviwe, tumbled out. They were all wearing yellow kit with the words *Clay Cow Cheese* on the back.

Potso saw me. He was wearing his choir shirt that Mrs. Jafta had recently made for all the choir members. I also noticed he had on new trousers and he grinned a bit shyly at me because he knew that I knew he was wearing new trousers. He walked over to me with his hands in both pockets.

"Hey," I said, also feeling strangely shy. I handed him something I'd wrapped in old newspaper. "I got this fixed for you."

He unwrapped his old cell phone and stared at it for a few moments. "Hayi man!" he said.

"I had a bit of extra money so I put some airtime in," I said.

"But will it work? Will it ring if I get a phone call?"

"It'll ring," I promised. "I tested it with Mr. Tshezi."

THE GRAND OPENING

Mr. Retief tapped the mic and said in a deep voice: "Can everybody hear me? You guys at the back?" I was standing behind the rows of chairs with Potso, Jude, Aviwe, Mawili and Prince waiting for the grand opening to begin, and we cheered and each gave him a thumbs up to show him that we could.

The chairs were only for the grownups. Lots of farmers were there, Mrs. Viljoen and Auntie Shirley from the library, our teachers and people from the municipality. Also Coach Nontso, Jimmy Klaasenss, Mr. Tshezi and Aviwe's dad.

My grandmother sat at the end of a row at the very front with a baby asleep over her shoulder.

One of the things my father did with his first salary was to put my grandmother on a taxi that went through to Kokstad so she could get her eyes tested. She had a small operation and returned a few days later with new spectacles.

When she got home, and could see, she took one look at our house and demanded new linoleum on the floor, new tin for the roof, and ceiling boards. She scrubbed the black smoke off the walls and painted them with a big tin of *Plascon Wall and All* that she got at a discount price from Mr. Retief's co-op. She also told my father to buy a load of concrete bricks and start building me a small bedroom at the back of the house. The foundations had been dug, the concrete bricks delivered, but, because my father could only work on weekends, progress on the building was slower than I liked. There was even talk of a small indoor bathroom with a toilet.

The next thing she did was march next door to Sis' uNomazizi and tell her that she wasn't to send her baby to the daycare behind the Methodist church anymore. She, my grandmother, was going to look after that baby herself during the days while Sis' uNomazizi was at work. Sis' uNomazizi was so grateful that she burst into tears.

It's nice having a baby in the house. Her name is Sinovuyo. She can't walk yet, but she pulls herself up against my grandmother's bed, and, if she hears music, she bounces up and down on her fat little legs in time to the beat. When she sees me, she buries her head in my grandmother's lap and turns her smiley face to peep at me.

"I want to welcome you all here today," said Mr.

Retief into the microphone. "To the opening of the Clay Cow Cheese factory." Everybody clapped and cheered and Mrs. Viljoen stood up, holding the clay cow I'd made in the air with both hands like a trophy. Everyone laughed and applauded even louder and the photographer I recognized from the Kokstad Advertiser got down on one knee and went *clickclickclickclick* with his camera.

"Now in honor of the two young boys who started this whole thing...Boipelo and Potso, where are you?" He put his hand up to shield his eyes from the sun and scanned the crowd. I felt Mawili's hand on my back as he shoved me forward. Potso and I looked down at the ground, smiling shyly and looking at each other out of the corner of our eyes. Our friends leaped around us, patting us on our backs and yelling like we were superstars.

"In honor of these two young boys..." Mr. Retief repeated over the noise..."I am going to ask Mrs. Seku, Boipelo's grandmother, and Mrs. Sebetso, Potso's mother, to come and do the unveiling for us."

My grandmother handed the sleeping baby to Sis' uNomazizi who sat beside her and got up. She waved her hands in the air and some of the women in the audience started ululating.

"Ha la la la la la la la-a-a!"

My own grandmother and Potso's mother went arm in arm to the front and together they tugged at the corner of the big white sheet and it fell in a crumpled heap at their feet to reveal a big yellow sign with the logo of the clay cow.

Everyone went crazy: clapping, cheering, dancing and waving their arms in the air. Potso nudged me and pointed to our school principal who was sitting very upright in his suit and clapping with one hand up and the other tapping his palm very politely.

After everyone had quieted a bit, Mr. Retief continued: "Boipelo and Potso are not the only talented young people in Cedarville. Many of you will remember that four months ago, a talent contest had to be canceled in this village because of unfortunate circumstances..." He waited for the laughter to die down.

"But I am glad to see that Mr. Sibaya from the Department of Arts and Culture has returned to our village today as an honored guest." Mr. Sibaya got up from the front row and bowed to the crowd. There was more cheering and ululating.

"We hope that he will be persuaded to stay behind after the performance for something to eat." Much more laughter ensued.

"So I thought it would be a good idea today when we are celebrating to sit back and enjoy the many talented youngsters of Cedarville. Today is not a competition. We are just here to have fun. So please give a round of applause to...the drum majorettes!" Mr. Retief lumbered off the stage and a whole crowd of girls in short white skirts and blue tops clopped on in their bright white boots.

I looked down the row of my friends and saw Sesi. She was also wearing her new choir shirt. She must have sensed I was looking at her, because she turned her head and smiled at me. I whipped my head back to look straight at the stage again. I wanted to swallow, but didn't want her to see me do it, or she'd know I was nervous. So I waited until I was certain she was no longer looking at me.

You would think that since "project paperclip" and the fact that I'd accidentally organized the re-opening of a cheese factory, I'd have got braver and found a way to talk to her. But it hadn't happened. I still felt like I'd be a stupid gobbling turkey if I opened my mouth, so I hardly spoke to her.

I saw her almost every day. When Mkhul' uGaba went to the TB hospital, where he stayed for many months, Sesi came every day to fill the bowl at his gate with clean water and put out pap for the stray dogs. Sometimes I helped her by washing the bowls, but I couldn't string proper sentences together, like a conversation; I could only manage words like "Hello," "Thanks," or "Do you think this bowl is clean enough?" I didn't know how I was ever going find the courage to say more.

The drum majorettes finished their act and the Under 15s soccer team followed them onto the stage, wearing their yellow kit. They were going to do tricks with a soccer ball—but the ball had disappeared. Someone ran to Mam' uSebetso's van to look for it.

While we waited patiently, the *Piet-my-vrou* called again from somewhere up in the big gum trees. The call was clear, sharp and sweet and everyone turned their heads to look for it, but it sat so still in the high branches that I doubt anyone spotted it.

Then a new sound...*dootle-do-do, dootle-do-do*—
a mobile phone rang right next to me. Potso nearly
jumped out of his skin. All our friends laughed as he
scrabbled in his trouser pocket and pushed random
buttons trying to answer it. He turned his back on us
and walked, trying to look casual, over to where the
cars were parked, to talk to the mysterious caller in
private.

I followed him and so did Sesi.

"Mkhul' uGaba," he said as he put the phone back in
his pocket. And Sesi gave a little gasp and put her hand
to her mouth.

"He's fine. He got permission to leave the hospital
to come to the opening today. The taxi dropped him at
the shop but he needs someone to help him walk down
here because he doesn't have a lot of strength."

"But why did he phone you?" I couldn't believe the
coincidence.

Potso laughed. "He got my number off those posters that are still up outside the café."

"I'll go," said Sesi.

"No, let me do it. You and Potso have to sing just
now. You have to be here—you're doing the solo. You
might not get back in time."

"The choir is only at the very end. I'll be back in time."

Potso had another idea. "I will ask my mother to
fetch him in the van then he won't have to walk at all."

"Then I'll definitely be back in time," said Sesi.

Potso went to whisper to his mother, who was

sitting next to Mrs. Jafta watching the Under 15s while they flicked, kicked and tapped a ball between them. She whispered something to Mrs. Jafta who looked at her watch and nodded.

Sesi and Mam' uSebetso drove off together.

SOLO

Act after act followed: dancing, singing, more soccer tricks, stick fighting...and at last I heard a car coming— but it wasn't the white van. It was a red bakkie. Mkhul' uGaba, wearing a knitted hat and a coat and leaning on a walking stick, got out of the passenger seat and walked slowly and carefully towards the stage. Mrs. Jafta saw him and immediately vacated her seat so he could sit down. She squatted down beside him and they had a whispered conversation. I could see she was worried because she kept standing up to look up the road, just as I was doing. But there was no sign of that white van.

There was some more singing, a short fashion show— and still Sesi did not return.

"And now for the final act," Mr. Retief spoke into the mic. "The choir led by Mrs. Jafta."

Mrs. Jafta came quickly to the back where I stood

with Potso.

"You'll have to do the solo," she said to him. "Mkhul' uGaba got a lift with that red bakkie, and I don't know what's happened to Sesi."

Potso did the solo fine. But his voice was just starting to break, so he couldn't get the high notes as easily as Sesi would have done. If she'd been there, she would have made those notes sing clean and clear as a bird calling the summer from high up in a gum tree.

Just as the choir sang the final verse together, *"'Twas grace that brought us safe so far and grace will lead us home..."* Sesi arrived.

She squeezed through the crowd of people standing at the back to stand next to me.

"We couldn't find him," she whispered. "Potso said he was outside the shop, but we drove everywhere..."

"He's here." I pointed to where the old man sat in his coat and hat with both of his big bony hands resting on his walking stick. "He got a lift with someone else."

Sesi closed her eyes with relief.

There was a lot of laughter coming from the audience seated in the chairs. Luvo was trying to get his wheelbarrow up onto the stage, but the big cardboard box it was carrying kept falling out. Some of his friends came to help him pick it up and plonk it down.

Mr. Retief took the mic again. "Just one more thing, then we can have tea," he said, as he took out a pocket knife and ripped open the cardboard box. "We have T-shirts here, one for every participant in today's talent show. We've counted very carefully so I don't want any-one grabbing. **Only** participants." He glared at us kids at the back of the audience, then he held up a bright yellow T-shirt with the clay cow cheese logo on the front. On the back, it read *Say Cheese!* in white lettering.

After everyone had gone up to get a T-shirt, there was one left. Mrs. Jafta, who'd been helping to distrib-ute, pointed at Sesi where she stood beside me—but Sesi shook her head, looked fiercely in front of her—and would not go up.

SONG

After the tea, I walked home with Potso, Jude, Mawili and Prince.

We had never seen so much food as we saw that day on those big silver trays, and it was all we could talk about: sausages, little pies, cakes, cubes of cheese on sharp sticks, small tomatoes and meatballs. Jude said he thought he ate fifteen sausages and Mawili told us he only ate cake until one of the farmer's wives put her hand out and said, "That's the seventh slice of granadilla cake you've taken, young man. You are going to be sick." We teased him by repeating it over and over in her funny accent.

My own tummy was tight as a skin stretched over a cowhide drum. A farmer's wife stood near the table to make sure that we didn't put too much food in our pockets, but I did sneak in a chicken drumstick wrapped in a yellow paper napkin.

SONG

We were walking up Station Road towards the Town Hall when something made me look behind me. Sesi was walking alone.

I fell back, walking slowly so that she caught up with me.

"Hey, Boi," she said and I saw that she'd been crying.

"Hey, Sesi."

I didn't know what to say to her.

"I wish I had something to give you," I said at last, but she looked at me confused. "I mean like one of those yellow T-shirts or something." But I knew this kind of sadness needed something much more than a yellow T-shirt.

"I'm not upset about the T-shirt."

"No?"

"I just..." Her eyes filled with tears, and I could see that she was irritated by the way she wiped them away so fiercely with the back of her hand. "I just...really, really wanted to sing today." She wiped her nose. I never imagined Sesi would cry. She was always so calm and certain.

"I'm sorry too. I really wanted you to sing."

"It's what I love. Singing."

"I love it when you sing too."

I was having this conversation with her and another part of me was thinking, "You're talking! You're talking to Sesi Jafta!" I remembered learning to ride a bike and the feeling I had when suddenly I got it and the bike stayed upright! It moved forward! It was that feeling.

"Well," she said carefully, "I wanted to sing for you."

I hardly dared to look at her.

"For me?"

"You've done something, Boi. Something impossible …but wonderful.

"No, I didn't. I just a made mess. And then it all just kind of happened by accident. I didn't know it was going to turn out like this."

She shook her head. "Something like this doesn't happen by accident. Somebody has to make it happen."

"Well, it wasn't just me. There was Potso, Mrs. Viljoen, Coach Nontso, Sis' uDana, Mr. Tshezi, Mr. Retief, Musa Masela from the *Sunday Times*…"

Sesi just laughed and shook her head.

There are small trees all the way up Station Road and they were covered in new green spring leaves. Suddenly, right above our heads, another Piet-my-vrou called. Just once.

Piet-my-vrou.

I looked up and for the first time in my life, I saw it: it was nothing special, just a medium-sized bird with a cinnamon chest. And suddenly, wonderfully, just as Mrs. Jafta had told us as choir practice that evening many months ago, out of the blue sky, it happened and I saw what I could do.

"I do actually have something to give you," I said. "Something you might like." And I held out my hands— one cupped over the other to hold the precious thing inside.

"What is it?" she asked and bent over my hands.

"It's the *Piet-my-vrou*. His song. I...er...I think you might like it. "

She put her own hands over mine and very gently she took the song from me and held it against her heart.

Then, just like that, we held hands—I held hers, she held mine—all the way up Station Road, past the church, past the library, past the town hall and the shop. All the way along Main Road to Khorong Koali Park.

And all the birds sang.

THE END

PIET-MY-VROU ?
IMIFINO?
LADUUUUMA ?

GLOSSARY

amalongwe *(um-ah-lon-gweh)*: dried cow pats used for fuel

amaphara *(um-ah-par-ah)*: petty thieves

amasi *(ah-ma-si)*: sour milk, also known as maas

doek: a cloth or scarf used to tie up women's hair

eish *(aiy-sh)*: an expression used for many emotions: surprise, disappointment, affection etc.

enkosi *(n-koh-si)*: thank you

ewe *(e-weh)*: yes

hambani *(hum-bah-ni)*: off you go (plural)

hawu *(how)*: an expression of surprise, like "Oh"

haibo *(hi-yi-boh)*: wow

GLOSSARY

hayi *(hah-yee)*: no

hok: an enclosure for chickens

imifino *(imi-feeno)*: edible wild greens

indoda *(in-doh-da)*: man

inkwenkwe *(in-kwen-kweh)*: a young man

khaki-bos *(car-key-bos)*: a weed that has a pithy stem

kwedini *(kweh-dee-nee)*: a young boy

laduuuuma *(lah-duuuu-mah)*: laduma means goal. The word is often stretched out

Legavaan *(Leg-a-vaan)*: a species of large lizard

magintsas *(Mah-ghin-tsahs)*: gangsters

Makhulu *(Ma-kooh-looh)*: big mother or grandmother

Malume *(Ma-luh-meh)*: Uncle

Mkhulu *(Mm-kooh-looh)*: The word is a shortened version of *Tat'omkhulu* that means big father or grandfather.

mntwan'am *(m-twah-naam)*: My child. Used as a term of great affection

molo *(moh-loh)*: Hello. This is an isiXhosa greeting, borrowed from the English greeting "morning" and from the Afrikaans greeting "môre"

GLOSSARY

Nkosi-yam *(Nkor-si-yum)*: Thank you or my Lord.

nxa: an exclamation of displeasure. The word is made with a click with the tongue where the air comes out of the side of the mouth

pap *(pup)*: porridge made from maize meal

Piet-my-vrou *(Piet-may-fro)*: Afrikaans word for a type of cuckoo (which translates as Piet-my-wife)

Sisi *(See-see)*: Sister. Sometimes shortened to Sis'. Used as a respectful term for a young woman

Siyabulela *(See-yah-buh-leh-lah)*: We are thankful

stokvel *(stock-fell)*: a group that meets regularly to save money.

suka *(suh-ka)*: Go away

Thula thu thula mntwan'am thula sana *(Tooh-lah)*: a lullaby that means "keep quiet my child"

umblaselo *(om-blah-seh-loh)*: Traditional pants and waistcoat patched with bright colours and braid

voetsek! *(foot-sek)*: A rude term meaning "get lost"

vuvuzela: a long plastic trumpet that makes one, low note. Used at soccer matches in South Africa

Yiz' apha *(Yee-zah-pah)*: Come here

AUTHOR'S NOTES

APARTHEID

From 1948 until 1994, South Africa had a system of government known as apartheid. Apartheid is an Afrikaans word that means "apartness" or "the state of living apart." For 46 years the white Nationalist Party of South Africa enforced laws that were based on two main features: white minority rule and the separation of its black, white, Indian and Coloured citizens.

Apartheid laws made sure that members of these racial groups were not allowed to live, operate businesses or own land outside of their designated areas. So children of different races went to separate schools; sick people got treated in separate hospitals; people didn't share transportation, living areas, leisure places or even stand in the same lines. Many black people were forced to live in the poorest areas of South Africa called "the Homelands" and they traveled from there to work in mines, industries and farms that were owned by white people. The apartheid government tried to convince the world that the system meant separate but equal but in reality only white people benefited and black citizens were severely discriminated against and lived lives of unrelenting hardship and poverty.

Many of the problems faced by Boi and Potso's families and neighbors in this story will have their origins in this period of South African history.

Because of this inequality, many people resisted apartheid. And eventually in 1994, after pressure from the international community, as well as growing internal resistance from the anti-apartheid movement, South Africa held its first democratic elections. The African Nationalist Congress (the ANC) under Nelson Mandela was voted into power.

THE RECONSTRUCTION AND DEVELOPMENT PROGRAM (RDP)

One of the new programs initiated by the new ANC government was the Reconstruction and Development Program (the RDP). It was hoped that this program would correct some of the injustices of the past and help to alleviate poverty. The aim was to build houses and make sure that people had access to clean water, electricity and healthcare. Between 1994 and the early 2000's, over two million cheap houses were built with government subsidies.

Boi's house in Khorong Koali Park was built as part of this program. Some people have criticized the program for the poor quality of the houses. Critics also say that the housing is dreary and looks very similar to houses that were built during the time of apartheid. One of the main criticisms is that houses were built in areas where there was not enough work to sustain the people who live in them. Unemployment remains one of South Africa's biggest challenges, and the village of Cedarville is no different from hundreds of other small South African towns in this regard.

SOCIAL GRANTS

To try and off-set this problem of unemployment, the ANC government also initiated a system of social grants to poor and vulnerable people. People who are unemployed, pensioners or mothers in need of child support can apply for monthly cash transfers. It is this small amount of money that sustains Boi's family. His grandmother goes to collect her pension each month from the South African Social Security Agency (SAS-SA) office in Matatiele.

LANGUAGES

South Africa is a country with eleven official languages; most people can speak at least two quite fluently. The languages that are most spoken are isiZulu and isiXhosa. In the area of the Eastern Cape where Cedarville is situated, people speak isiXhosa, Sesotho (pronounced *Sesootoo*), English and Afrikaans. Both Boipelo and Potso have Sesotho names but they speak isiXhosa fluently. The names that they use for

Mkhul' uGaba and Mam' uZungu are isiXhosa names. Mrs Viljoen, at the Cedarville shop speaks a strange mixture of English and isiXhosa that is known as *funagalo*.

isiXhosa is famous for its click sounds. Watch this YouTube video if you want to pronounce the word isiXhosa correctly: https://www.youtube.com/watch?v=Trq_gle1vO4

If you want to greet someone in isiXhosa you say *molo*.

Sesotho is the official language of Lesotho, a small mountain kingdom situated near to Cedarville on the Eastern side of South Africa. This language also has some click consonants. If you wanted to greet someone in Sesotho, you say *dumela*.

THANKS

This is a story with two lives. It was first published in a much shorter form, titled *Shoot for the Moon*, in 2008, by Hodder, as part of an African Reader series. When the copyright lapsed, Hilary Kromberg suggested I re-work the idea, (thanks Hil), and the result is the book you now hold in your hands.

For nearly 50 years of my life, wherever I went in the world, the area around Cedarville was "home" to me. For this I thank my mum and dad, Kip and Val Anderson, with all my heart. Thanks espcially to Kip for reading early drafts and advising on names and phrasing.

Thanks too to Kyle MacDonald who really did trade a red paper clip for a house, and who gave me permission to use his idea in this tale.

I'm also grateful to Cathy Green and Mrs Mfene from Cedarville for taking me back to hidden corners of the village and reminding me of the resilience of the people who live there.

Xolisa Guzula and Sinovuyo Mcunukelwa helped hugely in straightening out my wonky isiXhosa phrasing. I'm so grateful to them. If there are mistakes, it's my fault, not theirs.

Thanks too to Kath Magrobi, Liz Mattson and Moraig Peden for being my trusty early readers. It's a big ask to get someone to read an early draft and I'm so very grateful for their insights and generosity.

Thanks too to Dylan Ward who loves this story and tried valiantly to come up with a title.

My grateful thanks also go to Karen Vermeulen for the cover and illustrations and to Jessica Powers from Catalyst Press for agreeing to publish it and for working so hard to bring African stories to the world.

I also owe a debt of gratitude to an unknown man who attended a choir performance at Hilton College in 2019 and who presented a choir member with the *Piet-my-vrou* award in his cupped hand. I have tried so hard to find out who you are and get your permission to re-use this lovely poetic gesture. I hope you won't mind that it has been used here to help Boi to win Sesi's heart.

And finally, love and thanks always to Anton, Davie, and Simon.